UNDONE

ANDREA HURTT

Piece Of Pie Publishing

Piece Of Pie Publishing

11923 NE Sumner ST Ste 826515

Portland, OR 97220-9601

Cover by: MG Designs

Editor: C.A. Szarek

Undone

I can't live without you
I can't love without you
I will die without you

For my Family and Friends -
Thank you for standing by my side as I brave this new world. Your
support means more to me than you all ever know!

Shout out to the SPN Family...

Without you, this wouldn't be possible. You were the first to buy my debut novel and tell the world about me!

Chapter One

"Breathe. Just breathe." Grace took a deep breath when she entered the community hall's recreational room.

This was where she was going for her life-changing event?

The lights were bright, old harsh fluorescent tube bulbs. The room smelled like a locker room.

She took in the less-than-impressive view.

The bleachers were closed and pushed up against the walls, giving the place a large cavernous feel. If anyone yelled, it would echo off the walls.

That made Grace smile.

The slice of joy only lasted seconds.

Her new costar was about ten feet away, bouncing a red dodgeball like it was a basketball.

She cringed inside.

Those balls were made of nightmares!

"Gracie! You're here! It's about damn time! We can't get started without you. Hey! Catch!" The good looking, well-built twenty-one-year-old man threw the ball at her.

She stepped out of the way before it could collide with her.

The flying red rubber hit the wall behind her, only to roll back her way.

Grace continued to ignore it, moving closer to not only him but the others in the room.

"Seriously, Grace. Would it really hurt that much if it hit you?" Charles crossed his bare muscled arms over his chest, looking at her with mock disapproval.

If you only knew.

She forced a smile and stood by the other actors. Grace, for all her name implied, had always been clumsy.

In middle school, they'd given her the nickname, *'Graceless'*. One time in gym class, she'd tried to dodge one of those red balls. She'd slipped and broken her left arm when she'd hit the wooden floor.

She'd screamed like the world had ended, and everyone laughed.

The horrible teasing was born.

That was the day she'd lost her voice, not just physically, but emotionally. She'd become an introvert, caving in on herself.

If Grace talked with no one, no one could hurt her.

Years later, the theater had helped change all that. Taking on characters, *becoming* someone else, her whole body changed.

She had poise and grace she'd never had before.

Her new addiction.

She always needed more.

"Everyone, please take your seats, I don't care where. Just sit and I'll pass out the scripts," Jason, the man in charge said.

He was an amazing man with a vision. At six-foot, five inches, his height alone made her uncomfortable. His sun-bleached hair and copper-tone skin shouted he spent more time outside than in a dark theater.

When he smiled, and those pearly white teeth shone, it set her at ease.

Jason had been on a massive search throughout the theater communities everywhere for actors looking to spread their wings.

He needed people that could act, sing, and dance and weren't afraid to leave their homes for an extended period.

That was what'd caught her eye and motivated Grace to drive the long distance to audition.

She took a seat next to her new costar and tried to push back memories she didn't need at the moment.

She *had* to focus.

The script in her hand took on a permanent curve because she kept rolling it and squeezing, then unrolling and smoothing it out.

Her nerves were getting the best of her.

I still can't believe I am here. This is really happening. Mom, I'm doing it. I'm doing this for you.

Charles bumped her shoulder, bringing her back to the moment. "Are you ready for your life to change?" he whispered in her ear, his breath warm from his earlier exertion with the damned red ball.

※ ✦

TWO WEEKS EARLIER, SHE'D DRIVEN THIRTEEN HOURS FROM Denver to Minneapolis for an audition. Grace drove because, in the Midwest, if it was fourteen hours or fewer, it was drivable.

At the Minneapolis Convention center, she'd walked the long corridor that led to her final destination. She pushed open the heavy door to the auditorium; her breath caught in her throat when she took in the surrounding scene.

The auditorium was beautiful, warm in its shades of soft green. It held over three thousand seats, and as she listened to the older gentleman singing from the center of the large stage; the dynamic acoustics swept her away.

Is he really that great of a performer, or is it the room configuration helping him along? Will I sound that good? Can I even come close?

She glanced side to side, seeing hundreds of hopeful actors, ranging in all ages and sizes. She was really there, auditioning for a musical, without even knowing the title.

What if it's in a range I can't sing in? Or, there are no characters in my age bracket? What if I step on some poor actor's foot and break his toes?

All her previous childhood insecurities came flooding back, and she tripped over her own shoes walking down the aisle towards the stage.

Luckily, Grace didn't hit the ground, and strong hands caught her; helped steady her.

"Woah, there. You gotta be more careful. You're not supposed to break a leg until the day we go on stage together." His voice was as strong as his arms, yet youthful.

She looked into the most intense, beautiful brown eyes, rimmed with hints of gold. She studied his face, from the stumble on his chin to his soft pink lips; noting the bottom one was fuller than the top.

He had a quirky smile, or maybe it was cocky?

His cheekbones were sharp, but not overly so, just enough to give his face a slender look. His hair was dark at the roots, then lightening to a sweet golden sunshine blond.

However, he couldn't be over twenty-one.

He was *stunning*.

His smile deepened, showing perfectly straight, white teeth, causing her heart to slam in her chest.

It was then the words he'd spoken hit her.

"We?" she asked.

"We're clearly the best choices to play Maddie and Louis," he said, vanity filled his voice like his previous words had.

"Maddie and Louis? Did... Did you say, Maddie and Louis?" Her heart had been pounding *before*. Her hands shook at his casual drop of the character's names.

"That *is* what I said. Do you know the characters, then?"

"Oh my God, yes! *The Splendids*? He's doing *The Splendids*, the longest-running off-Broadway show in history? That's my all-time favorite musical!" She was freaking out. It'd always been a dream of hers to portray Maddie, but at twenty-nine, she was getting too old to play the role of a seventeen-year-old.

The younger man stuck out his hand. "I'm Charles. And you are?"

"Screwed."

He said something, but she missed his retort.

"Well, that was a wasted trip," she grumbled.

Charles' brow creased in confusion.

She oddly felt inclined to tell him why she was suddenly so disappointed.

"I'm too old to play Maddie."

"Okay, let's back up a moment. I'm Charles, and you are?"

Heat suffused her cheeks. She was ashamed of herself for her lack of manners. "Sorry. I'm Grace."

"Well then, *Grace*. Let's get you signed in to audition." He took a few steps forward, before looking back to see if she was following.

She hadn't moved.

Charles shrugged and his hands were palms up. "Aren't you coming?"

"Didn't you hear what I just said? There's no point. They're not gonna offer the lead role to an old lady."

"If you're an old lady, I'm Moses. You know what, you'll never know if you don't try."

"Seriously? You're gonna give me that stupid saying? Clichés are death; just don't go there." The muscles in Grace's back went slack.

"That stupid saying is as true today as it was when... well, whoever said it first. You'll live the rest of your life wondering if you *could've* had the role if you'd only had the courage to try. Come on, Grace. Step up. If you don't go, I don't go. You wouldn't want to ruin my career too, do you?" He smiled again, and she had a feeling he often got his way. "Really, Grace, what do you have to lose?"

"Besides my dignity?" she asked.

"Well, you did literally fall into my arms."

"Oh, all right. You win."

They went the rest of the way down the aisle, and when Charles offered her his arm; she took it.

Better not to trip again when she stepped closer to where the director was sitting.

The tall man was in the front row, along with four other people; three women and one other man. They had a table placed in front, covered with resumes and headshots, where they seemed to be deep into discussions.

Grace stepped up, pulled her profile folder from her handbag and handed it to the first person, an older lady with beautiful short Easter-egg-pink curled hair. "We'll call you when it's your turn. Just join the talent in the upper-tier seats."

The others at the table didn't even glance her way.

Not that they needed to, she really didn't matter until she was up on the stage.

Her mother had drilled proper etiquette into her and not being acknowledged dropped her spirits.

Grace felt defeated already.

"Hey, it's gonna be all right. Shall we join the others up in the nosebleeds?" Charles reminded her he was by her side.

She'd barely heard him, lost in her disappointment.

He took her hand and led her to two empty seats in the highest tier of the auditorium.

She was grateful for this guy, helping her out in those first minutes in the theater.

She enjoyed having him sit beside her, but soon enough they called him to the front.

Grace gave his thigh a pat, quietly thanking him for his

support. Although he wasn't always on stage, he never returned to her.

She glanced at her watch.

It's only been three hours, but it feels like forever.

She was one of the last, which she was grateful for.

If I was just a few years younger, I'd have a real chance at this role. I swear, less than a third of these actors have ever heard of this musical, let alone known any of the songs.

Grace knew it intimately.

Her mother had introduced as a child. They had an old vinyl LP of the London production from the mid-1980s. They played it whenever they could, dancing and singing along as they cleaned house and did laundry.

Who needed the television when you had The Splendids *to listen to!*

As a child, she'd envisioned what the sets would be like, the costumes, and the magic. She'd hoped one day to see it performed live, but to date, hadn't had an opportunity.

When they finally called Grace, it felt like an eternity walking the distance from the back of the theater, down the long-declining isle.

She took her first step onto the hardwood floor of the stage, filling her lungs with air, and allowing Maddie to take over.

Her body relaxed, like that of a youthful girl in love. She felt seventeen at that moment; she reached for it.

Grace closed her eyes and released the breath.

The music began and a beautiful male voice started off the song.

> *"Once the sky was new,*
> *Once the spring had come*
> *Once the scene was set for a night of fun.*
> *The stars adorned the night*
> *Then clarity was sung:*

> *It was true.*
> *It was true.*
> *It was true."*

IMAGINING ALL THE TIMES SHE'D DANCING AROUND THE HOUSE with her mother to that song, her feet moved her to the center of the stage, coming up to the man who was singing.

Without taking a moment to see his face, Grace allowed him to take her into his arms in a tender embrace. He turned her away to face the audience, his arms wrapping around her waist protectively. In the breath she took before dazzling the audience with her lines, Grace's nose received a hint of heady musk from the man holding her so lovingly in his arms.

It was oddly comforting. She relaxed into him without thought.

She sang the lyrics to the crowd when they swayed back and forth with the music in perfect time.

> *"Once the fun died down,*
> *Once you went astray,*
> *Once I ran to hunt things so far away.*
> *The stars upon the night,*
> *Disappeared from sight:*
> *It was true.*
> *It was true..."*

THE MAN BEHIND HER SLIPPED HIS WARM HANDS ACROSS HER ribcage so he could grab her waist. The heat of his touch lingered when he lifted her off the ground as they danced, spinning around.

He gently set her down, the music fading away; she turned to face her Louis.

Still completely in the mind of Maddie, she placed a tender hand on his cheek, not surprised when his larger hand covered hers.

She'd been so wrapped up in being Maddie; she took a moment staring into his intense brown eyes to realize one very important thing.

Grace was wrapped in Charles' arms.

Chapter Two

IT WAS JUST another audition in another city. This time, it was one show Charles already had the lead role in. His agent had assured him the character was his, if he wanted it. He'd been on the fence about it; this was just a little off-Broadway show.

It might be a very famous play, but will it be worth my time?

He was already famous in his own right and had been offered roles before, more prestigious shows than this one, but he still had decided to see if it was worth his time.

Charles sat in the uncomfortable green padded seats in the Minneapolis Convention Center auditorium, watching people come and go.

Most of the actors there to audition were sitting in the back; he'd placed himself in the very middle. He didn't see any point in going to the back when he was constantly going on the stage to interact with the female actors and to occasionally sing again.

They had other actors trying out for Louis, probably as a backup, or as an understudy, in case he didn't want the role. Which was highly likely, at the rate they were going.

His eyes had been on stage, watching each female audition, trying to see if he could envision them as his costar.

Not one felt right.

If my costar and I don't have some chemistry, the show reflects that, which reflects off me. That's not acceptable.

A tingle down his spine urged Charles to look over his shoulder.

His heart caught in his throat as a woman stepped into the theater.

He couldn't look away as she stopped, taking in the sight before her. He couldn't help but do the same.

Her hair was chestnut and fell in soft curls about halfway down her back; one full piece was over her shoulder, trying to cover part of her chest.

He couldn't see the lines of her face, the theater was too dark, but he could tell she was beautiful.

Charles held his breath and scanned over her light pink blouse. The top two buttons strained slightly because of her full breasts. Her jeans were black and fitted nicely over long, shapely legs.

She was tall, yet wore black character heels, the dance shoes all the women wore for stage dancing.

It impressed him that she'd thought to wear those for her audition. He had yet to see another actress in shoes that fit the events of the day.

She took a few timid steps forward, on her way to deliver her resume and headshot to the casting crew in front of the stage.

The woman kept her head forward, held with a dignity that impressed him.

However, as she neared, something in her face changed, a flash of fear, or apprehension, and she took a wrong step.

He jumped up; thankful he'd been sitting in the aisle seat and caught her as she went down.

Charles helped her to her feet and stared into the most beautiful blue-green eyes he'd ever seen.

A spark shot through him.

She's the one.

"Woah, there. You gotta be careful. You're not supposed to break a leg until the day we go on stage together."

They locked gazes, and Charles' heart raced.

She was beautiful, but not in a movie star way, like the girls he'd dated in the past, but like the girl-next-door, a guy wanted to spend the rest of your life with.

Her question broke his dreaming.

"We?"

He shook his head to clear his mind. "We're clearly the best choices to play Maddie and Louis." Charles could only hope she could sing and dance, but at that moment, it didn't matter.

The show doesn't matter.

Only this woman did.

"Maddie and Louis? Did... Did you say, Maddie and Louis?"

"That *is* what I said. Do you know the characters, then?"

"Oh my God, yes! *The Splendids?* He's doing *The Splendids*, the longest-running off-Broadway show in history? That's my all-time favorite musical!"

He could see the excitement across her face.

I need to know her name.

"I'm Charles. And you are?"

"Screwed."

Oh, I very much wish that, but not the way she means..

He could envision her long legs wrapped around his waist as he took her with a fierce passion she'd clearly never known.

His thoughts slipped out into words. "Not right now, but definitely later." He was a little disappointed she hadn't heard him. Charles almost missed what she said in return.

"Well, that was a wasted trip," she grumbled. "I'm too old to play Maddie."

He would not lose her for something as stupid as age. Besides, she looked to be the same age he was; twenty-one. Actors in their twenties played teen roles all the time.

"Okay, let's back up. I'm Charles, and you are?" He watched as a blush filled her cheeks. It sent waves of excitement through him. She'd gotten flushed so easily. He couldn't wait to make her blush again.

"Sorry. I'm Grace."

Grace? It suits her.

Aside from her fall, which had landed her in his arms, she was full of grace.

"Well then, *Grace*," he said her name with reverence. "Let's get you signed in to audition." He started down the incline to the front of the stage, but when he no longer felt the radiating heat of her presence, whirled. "Aren't you coming?"

"Didn't you hear what I just said? There's no point. They're not gonna offer the lead role to an old lady."

"If you're an old lady, then I'm Moses. But you know what, you'll never know if you don't try." He wasn't going to let her go that easily.

"Seriously? You're gonna give me that stupid saying. Clichés are death, just don't go there."

"That stupid saying is as true today as it was when... well, whoever said it first. You will live the rest of your life wondering if you *could* have had that role if you'd only had the courage to step up. Come on, Grace. Step up. If you don't go, I don't go. You don't want to ruin my career too, do you?"

He wasn't about to tell her that the role was already his, and her choice really wouldn't affect his career in the slightest.

It would only affect his heart, his soul.

Which might be worst.

"Really, Grace, what do you have to lose?"

"Besides my dignity?"

"Well, you did literally fall into my arms," he politely reminded her.

"Oh, all right. You win."

He offered her his arm and wouldn't take no for an answer. One way or another, he'd get her on that stage.

Hopefully, into his arms.

Charles stood beside her as she handed over her resume and headshot.

Her shoulders fell a little when no one acknowledged her other than the first attendant.

He tenderly ran his hand down the length of her soft bare arm, stopping only when he reached her hand, taking it into his own.

He felt that spark again, something pulling her to him.

Charles gave a gentle squeeze. "Hey, it's gonna be all right. Shall we join the others up in the nosebleeds?" He lifted his chin to indicate the large crowd in the back of the theater.

She just nodded and followed his lead.

He took her to the very back of the theater, so they could sit alone. Rather ironic for the reason he'd chosen the place he'd sat earlier seemed to no longer matter.

They sat there in silence, watching the auditions, listening to far too many people who could not sing.

Unfortunately, they called Charles back to the stage and he had to leave Grace behind.

She just patted his thigh, like they were old friends.

It feels so right. I just need to get her on stage. The off-stage chemistry is driving me mad, so I can only speculate what our onstage chemistry will be like.

One by one, the actors continued to file on and off the stage. Sometimes with him, sometimes without.

The crowd had gotten smaller and smaller until just a few people were still in the auditorium.

He'd tried to watch Grace, keep an eye on her as she waited for her turn, but he couldn't see her.

Charles had pulled Jason, the director, aside. "The actress, Grace, needs to be saved for last."

Jason nodded and went back to auditions.

He glanced at his watch as he stood backstage. It was nearly six in the evening. He'd been there almost ten hours.

They hadn't broken for lunch; there wasn't time. He needed to eat soon. He was hungry, and not just from the lack of talent coming across the stage.

Charles had been famous for almost half his life, and the monkey's auditioning for the play were a joke.

At this rate, he wanted nothing to do with the show.

He was just about ready to call it a night when they called *her* up.

Charles wasn't the one currently singing for Louis; he was standing off to stage left.

The moment they called Grace's name, his chest tightened; he needed to be the one she sang with.

He rushed to the male actor standing center stage, snatching the guy's arm and tugging him into the shadows of stage right. "I'll be singing with this one," he commanded.

"But, I'm..."

Charles squeezed the man's biceps harder, digging his nails into the soft flesh. "Step away, boy. She's mine."

Shock danced across the actor's face, but he nodded.

He smiled to himself and stepped into the spotlight. Then he sang.

> "*Once the sky was new,*
> *Once the spring had come*
> *Once the scene was set for a night of fun.*
> *The stars adorned the night*
> *Then clarity was sung:*
> *It was true.*
> *It was true.*
> *It was true.*"

HE SANG, AND SHE DANCED INTO THE CENTER OF THE STAGE, then came right to him. He opened his arms to take her in and Grace accepted him.

Charles took a raspy breath in anticipation, as he slid his hands across the smooth satin of her pink shirt to rest them on the sides of her perfect waist.

He turned her to face the audience, her soft back against his chest. His body reacted to the closeness of hers and he had to calm himself, but how?

His hands trailed her waist to meet in the center, his arms now wrapped around her.

He pressed his cheek to hers, feeling the heat of her skin, breathing in the sweet smell of her shampoo that still lingered on her hair.

She sang her lines to the crowd, and they moved back and forth with the music.

The love Maddie felt for Louis was so clear in her voice.

Grace astonished not only him but the remaining actors *and* the production team.

> *"Once the fun died down,*
> *Once you went astray,*
> *Once I ran to hunt things so far away.*
> *The stars upon the night,*
> *Disappeared from sight:*
> *It was true.*
> *It was true..."*

CHARLES' HANDS RELUCTANTLY LEFT THEIR RESTING PLACE, only to glide once again across her flat stomach, back to her sides. He gripped her tight and lifted her off the ground as they danced.

He spun them around, allowing her feet to touch the floor just before he spun her one last time so Grace could face him, their bodies moving perfectly together.

Charles held his breath when she reached up and put a warm hand on his cheek. His body responded before his mind could, and he placed his own over hers.

He stared deeply into her blue-green eyes, ready to whisk her away and devour her with the fervency he was flooded with.

In that breath, something was obvious.

She hadn't realized she danced and sang with *him* until then.

This was nothing more than another audition to her!

Grace must've been wrapped up in the character.

Everything he'd felt, the passion he'd thought they were sharing, was just *his*.

His alone.

Anger tore through him.

Charles had to get away before he said something he'd later regret.

He thanked Jason, the rest of the panel, and left the auditorium.

Chapter Three

"THREE HUNDRED CHANNELS and there's nothing to watch!"

Grace sat in her hotel room, flipping through the channels. She was a nervous wreck. Had this been any other play, it would just be another audition; not a big deal.

This one... it was her favorite musical. Something she'd shared with her mother before her passing.

It meant more to her than anyone could ever know.

"Oh, my." Her stomach grumbled, not wanting to be ignored any further. She put her hand over her abdomen.

She pulled on her jacket and she slipped on her shoes. Grace wanted to go eat at *Hell's Kitchen*. She'd seen a sign for the place and it was less than a fifteen-minute walk from her hotel.

Grace zipped her jacket, up to her chin. Although it was mid-April, the nights were still pretty crisp. She stepped out into the night air and headed west.

The restaurant was located in the basement of a building, decorated in black and red that gave it a dark ambiance. It suited her mood.

She should be so excited for the chance to be a part of the

show, but all her insecurities, her introvert-ness, came rushing back.

Grace tried not to think about them, as she checked in at the hostess station. "Table for one." She stepped up to the counter. She'd expected to see a young, attractive female at the counter, as was the prejudice of most restaurants, but was pleasantly surprised to be greeted by a handsome dark-haired man with a goatee. He was dressed all in black.

How appropriate for entering Hell.

"Oh, sweetie," he said. "A woman as beautiful as you shouldn't at a table alone! Can I get you a spot at the bar?"

She appreciated his concern, but it didn't help things. "I'd really prefer a table or booth where I can be alone. I've got some things to go over," she said, holding up her handbag, colorful folders sticking out of the top.

"Of course. Follow me." He led her to a dark corner, away from most of the buzz of the dining room.

Grace was grateful; it was exactly what she'd asked for, but it probably wasn't what was best for her psyche. She pulled out her folders and laptop and got to work while she waited for her server.

"Welcome to Hell. What can I get you?"

"Can I please get a Lucifer Lemonade and the ham and pear sandwich?" she asked the tiny blonde server, who nodded in acknowledgment before quickly walking away.

She felt completely alone at that moment.

Grace had worked so hard to get over her self-doubt, but it hit her in waves. Her dream was laid out before her, right at the tips of her fingers, yet it still felt out of reach.

She wasn't a trained singer—or dancer for that matter—even though she'd given a decent performance.

However, she was getting old.

In terms of acting careers, twenty-nine *was* old.

Grace was just finishing up her meal when her server brought over not only her bill, but a single red rose. She looked up at the young blonde waitress. She glanced around at the other patrons.

No one else has roses, so why do I?

Her server wore a grin. "I was just told to bring this to you, and let you know your bill was taken care of." She walked away, not allowing Grace to ask questions.

She sat there stunned, continuing to scan the room to see if anyone was glancing her way; any indication of who'd sent her this gift.

Grace found none.

It made her uncomfortable, so she grabbed her handbag and left the restaurant.

As Grace headed back to her hotel, she spotted a small liquor store. She wasn't a big drinker, and never had a drop once she was in a role, but she hadn't gotten a part yet, and really could use a little something.

She was pleasantly surprised to find her favorite sweet red wine in the little store. It could be difficult to find where she lived, so she was grateful to have a bottle to drink that night, and the next two following, if she was lucky.

She was the only child to a Lieutenant Colonel in the Army and had been taught to always be prepared. So when she'd booked her hotel, she'd done so for three nights; the time it would take if she made it to callbacks. She wasn't overconfident. Just wanted to be prepared.

Laughter filled the lobby as Grace entered the hotel. There was no one in the lobby but the two front desk clerks.

"It's coming from the pool," one of them said, sounding irritated, and pointing toward the hallway in front of her.

Curiosity got the best of her and she wanted to find out who was having so much fun. She stepped up to the wall of glass that held the pool behind it and saw quite a few of the other actors that'd been at auditions.

One of them waved a friendly hello before jumping out of the pool and running up to the door. She wrenched it open, the humidity hit Grace full on.

"Oh, hi! Um..." She struggled like she was trying to recall Grace's name.

That was funny, wasn't it? The auditions didn't encourage the exchanging of names.

"I'm Grace," she said to save her.

"I'm Lacey! Nice to meet you! So, you should totally come join us!"

Grace tried not to laugh at the younger girl, who couldn't be over eighteen, and her so 1990s vocabulary. "That's very thoughtful of you, but I'm just gonna head upstairs."

"Oh, yes, you should! To grab a swimsuit, or a non-see-through bra and panties." She leaned in closer then. "Maxine already shocked everyone with that little stunt."

That time she laughed, how could she not? It seemed to be something certain theater people liked to do, shock people.

It rarely affected other actors, but if there were regular people around, it always seems like a challenge to see who could get the most of an effect.

She glanced around the room, not looking for the half-naked girl, but just taking in the scene.

There was the hot tub in the corner. Her body cried out. She smiled at Lacey and accepted her invitation to join the crowd.

Back in her room, she poured herself a glass of sparkling red wine into a coffee cup and added the travel lid.

No one needs to know it's not coffee.

She was so glad she'd packed her swimsuit. She always brought it along on any trip, just in case. She drank an entire glass of wine while getting ready, to give herself a bit of courage. She refilled the cup, replaced the lid and headed back down to the pool area.

Grace let out a small sigh when she stepped in and saw the hot tub had only two people in it, and they were deep in conversation in the far left corner.

"Um, excuse me," she said.

They didn't even look at her, just kept talking to each other.

"Do you mind if I turn on the bubbles?" she persisted.

She tried three times to get their attention but got no response. So she did it anyway. She cranked the nob of the timer to twenty minutes and watched as they erupted.

Grace tried not to sigh out loud in pleasure as she stepped into the overly heated hot tub and sank in deep, keeping just her right arm out of the water and resting on the ledge. It held her paper cup of wine.

She listened to the laughter of everyone around her, wishing she could join in; it was clear quite a few of these actors knew each other.

Once again, she felt like she was all alone.

She didn't know anyone, and although she was always good at making friends, she felt out of place. There was no rhyme or reason for the funk she was in, other than she was doing it to herself.

Stop it, Grace!

From the pool room, there were large glass windows on the east side of the building. A few people walked by, even though it was getting late into the evening.

Grace couldn't help but smile when she saw a head full of sunshine blond hair come in to view.

He turned, looked into the room and stopped, a smile spread across his mouth. Charles waved hello. Then he held up one finger, as if to say just wait a minute, and he disappeared out of view.

The two other people in the hot tub left, and she was grateful to be alone. It only lasted a brief moment.

Three giggling girls ran and jumped in, splashing Grace.

She tried not to glare, but it was difficult to endure such rudeness.

She was about to get out and leave when one of the girls demanded her attention.

"Oh! I loved your audition today! Wow!" She turned to the girl next to her. "Did you see it? It was amazing. I was jealous! The chemistry between you and Charles was... wow."

Grace's cheeks flushed hot. No doubt she was as red as a tomato. Between the Lucifer's Lemonade at dinner and the two glasses of wine, mixed with the heat of the hot tub, she was more than feeling the effects of the alcohol.

She listened as they went on. She hadn't thought there were that many people left in the theater when it'd finally been her turn.

"I'd be shocked if those two don't end up with the lead roles," one girl said. "They looked like real lovers on stage."

"I wanna be his lover," another girl chimed in, bringing her hands up to her chest in a swoon-worthy sweep.

"Stand in line, honey," a good-looking man said, as he stepped in to join them.

The hot tub wasn't very large, although the sign posted on the wall beside it stated the capacity to be ten.

Grace was suddenly very crowded.

What had these people seen on stage? It'd just been an audition, Grace had just been playing a role.

Nothing more.

Even she couldn't deny, Charles was hot, and they had unusual chemistry she'd never experienced during an audition before. However, she'd been there to land a role in a play, not to find a relationship.

That was the *last* thing she wanted in her life.

The four others in the hot tub were still arguing over who had dibs on Charles. Someone admitted something about a crush for years, but Grace discarded most of the conversation.

She was done.

Physically and emotionally.

Exhaustion had finally won out.

Grace stepped out of the hot tub and wrapped a tiny pool towel around her waist, draping another over her shoulders. She grabbed her room key and cellphone from the small plastic table she'd set it on.

She pushed the *up* button of the elevator, and the doors opened.

Charles was there, wearing black swimming trunks and a gray shirt. His blond hair was tousled as if he'd dressed in a hurry, and sticking different directions.

It was cute.

He looked like he was freshly...

Grace shook her head to clear the thoughts away she did *not* want.

He smiled and stepped out.

She moved past him to enter the elevator.

"Where are you going?" he asked.

"To bed. It's been a long day," Grace said, wishing the doors would close faster to get her away from this distraction.

"But, I was just coming down to see you."

"I'm sorry. I'm sure I'll see you tomorrow."

The doors finally closed.

After a semi-cold shower, and a large glass of ice water, Grace curled up in her king-sized bed, ready for sleep to take her.

Instead of a restful night, she tossed and turned, unable to get comfortable. She was either too cold, or too hot. She flitted from one nightmare to the next.

One dream she kept coming back to, even after forcing herself awake, she'd fall right back into it when her eyes closed.

Grace dreamt about being in hell, the heat overwhelming, her discomfort part of the torment being dished out to her.

Thousands of roses surrounded her, the burning smell of them filling her nostrils and making her ill.

Then there was a tall man, standing over her. She couldn't see his face, only the outline of his lean, hard body. However, she could hear his voice, deep and resonating, saying the same words over and over.

"You will be mine, always."

Chapter Four

Why is this affecting me so badly?

It was just another audition! But Grace... she wasn't just another actress. There was something about her he couldn't resist.

What the hell!

He felt like he'd walked ten miles after leaving the theater, trying to clear his thoughts and calm his body.

I have to have her. She has to be my Maddie. If she doesn't get the role, I don't want Louis. She's the only one that fit.

He knew what he needed to do. Chemistry between actors was the most important thing.

Charles pulled his phone out of his back pocket and searched for Jason's number. There was no answer, so he tried again.

He continued to walk, his pace speeding up with each unanswered try.

After five times getting of Jason's voicemail, he left a message.

"Jason, call me. I need to discuss something important with you about your play."

He disconnected the line and kept strolling the downtown area.

Charles likely wouldn't hear from the man that night, but his agitation was getting the best of him.

He needed to calm down. His older brother was always giving him shit about having a short temper. He was easy to set off. Short fuse, and all that.

Charles took a deep breath and slowly let it out, trying to get his heart rate back to a normal level.

He contemplated the reasons these things upset him. It really was ridiculous.

I'm mad Grace hadn't felt the same fire on stage I had. But it wasn't her fault. It just might take her a bit longer to see what I see.

Everyone in that auditorium had seen the chemistry between them. They'd make an amazing Louis and Maddie. The show would be a success with them as the lead roles.

I know it.

Charles imagined them on stage; the roar of a thousand fans.

Wait. Was that Grace?

He caught movement out of the corner of his eye. He quickened his steps, opening the door to a building, and taking in what was before him.

There were three restaurants in the building.

Which one did she go to? If it was Grace I saw, she was alone. And no one should eat alone.

Charles walked into the *Melting Pot* and asked if a single woman, with Grace's description, had entered their establishment. He turned on all his charm with the young blonde hostess, hoping to get the help he needed. She took the bait, blushing at all his compliments.

It was for naught.

Grace wasn't there.

He went out the door and across the hall to *Star Pizza*, but again found no sign of her.

Back in the main entryway, he looked at the entrance for the last restaurant, *Hell's Kitchen*. There was an arrow pointing to a dark stairwell.

Charles loved the red and black walls, the black stairs leading down into the bowels of the building.

The color choice continued down into the reception area. Blood red walls and black furniture. Even the host stand had men that looked like they belonged in Hell.

His charm wouldn't help him this time. There was no young, pretty blonde to semi-seduce into getting information. He had to play things a bit differently. "Hi, I'm looking for my sister, cute brunette, about my height, alone."

The host, a man named Sam—according to his name tag—looked at him with disdain, before glancing back down at his table layout. "I'm sorry, but I don't have any single ladies sitting at tables."

"Maybe she's at the bar," Charles prompted, clenching his teeth.

"I'm sorry. Can't help you."

He tried to keep his temper in check. "Fine. I'll just check with her later." He whirled away, his hands in tight fists.

Seriously, though, is it that hard to let me know if she's here?

He had to try something different if he wanted to get what he needed. He headed back up the stairs, his step a little lighter.

As he had walked around downtown earlier, he'd seen a woman selling roses, just trying to make a few dollars.

If Charles could remember where she'd been, what block he had been on when he'd seen her, he'd buy a few flowers.

It took him about twenty minutes of running up streets and around corners until he finally found her.

"A rose for your lady?"

The woman had seen better days. Her clothing was ragged, her skin was dirty, and her shoes were worn down.

The roses she held were perfect.

"I only ask for a small donation," she pleaded as she held one rose out.

"I'll give you twenty if you give them all to me."

"Oh, thank you, thank you!"

He pulled his wallet out and watched her hungry eyes as he flipped through the wad of bills he'd tucked away. It was likely more money than she'd see in a lifetime.

Charles slipped out a hundred-dollar bill and handed it over. "Get something to eat. And maybe a place to sleep tonight."

The woman stood still, unable to form words, her mouth opening and closing like a fish out of water.

Charles walked away carrying the last of her precious roses.

He waited patiently outside the building for a small group of people to head down to the restaurant.

They would occupy Sam and he could slip around into the main dining room. He got back down to the bottom and watched the two hosts working.

One took a group to be seated, but headed off to the left.

Damn it! There's another dining room!

Charles hoped Grace was on the right side; it was the only one he could slip over to.

He stood off to the side watching, waiting until Sam took the new group to their table.

They also went off to the left dining room. That allowed him to move into the room on the right where he could search for Grace.

Why can't I find her?

He scanned the room a third time, and he finally saw her.

Tucked in a corner and almost hidden from view.

Grace was waiting for her check, ready to leave.

This isn't the time to approach.

The moment was lost.

A bright-smiled female server touched his shoulder. "Can I help you find someone?"

"Actually." Charles turned on his charm. "There's a beautiful lady sitting over there, alone. I want to pay for her meal and leave her this." He handed the rose to the girl.

"Oh! How sweet! That's my table, too. I can get the bill for you." She sauntered away, a bounce in her step.

He kept an eye on Grace as she put away her laptop and folders.

When the server returned, she held out the bill.

Without looking at the total, he handed her a fifty-dollar bill. "Keep the change. But don't tell her about me. It's our secret."

She smiled and nodded, then took off to present Grace with her rose.

Charles wanted to stay and watch but was afraid she'd see him and the game would be over. He headed back up the black steps and into the chilly April air.

He wasn't ready to embrace the solitude his hotel room offered, so he headed back over to the convention center. It was a short walk. Not more than ten blocks from the restaurant.

The doors were still unlocked—which surprised him—but he headed straight back for the auditorium.

Charles strode up the stairs like he owned the place. He stopped at center stage, staring out into the empty auditorium.

Charles! Charles! Charles!

He could hear the sound of thousands of girls screaming his name. It was something he still hadn't gotten used to.

He'd been a pop star since he was a kid, but the sound filled his head often. He shook the memories away. That wasn't what he wanted to hear.

I want to hear my name on her *lips.*

He danced across the stage, recreating the moves he'd shared with Grace, just hours before. Her sweet shampoo seemed to linger in the air.

Why do I want this? Why do I want you?

He'd done a handful of plays, worked with dozens of women, yet there was something about her, something about Grace.

"Hey! What're you doing? You can't be in here!" A loud masculine voice boomed from the back of the dark auditorium.

"Sorry," Charles called back. "I was finishing up from our auditions. But I'm heading out now."

The security guard watched him with suspicion as he made his way out of the auditorium.

He felt like the man was following him as he walked down the long hallway to exit the building.

His hotel was just across the street. It was nothing fancy; he just needed a bed to sleep on.

Sleep? Will I get any sleep if I can't get her off my mind?

Charles ran his hands through his hair, sending it in all directions.

What am I going to do? This isn't like me.

Sure, chemistry was important, but not enough that he should follow her around town. No, he wasn't following her.

We just happened to both be on the same street at the same time.

He continued to argue with himself, as he came up to the east side of the hotel. The bright lights from the pool room illuminated the sidewalk.

Charles heard the laughter from the other side and looked in.

Grace!

His heart raced. He waved but felt stupid as he did so.

One minute. Just wait for me!

He held up one finger, hoping she'd catch on. He had to keep himself in check and not sprint the distance to the front of the hotel.

Stay cool, man.

Charles fumbled with his keycard trying to get the door open in a hurry. All he wanted to do was get downstairs to see her, talk with her.

He tossed the remaining roses on the desk and rushed to change into swimwear.

Damn it! Stupid jeans! Shoes off first, idiot.

He almost fell when he tried to get out of his pants before taking off his shoes. He was half-way out the door, but something was missing.

A shirt. I'm walking through the lobby.

He grabbed a gray tee from his suitcase and pulled it over his head as he ran down the hallway to the elevator.

Hurry up, hurry up. It shouldn't take this long!

He kept pushing the *down* button as if it would make the elevator move faster.

The hotel was only three floors, but it was taking far too long. Charles was about to find the stairs when the door opened.

Patience wasn't one of his virtues and pressing buttons over and over wasn't helping.

It was just causing him more frustration. Trying to get himself in check, Charles began something his therapist recommended.

Breathe in... one, two, three, four. Hold. Breathe out... one, two, three, four.

The elevator came to a stop, and the doors opened. Before him stood a vision, of an exhausted, cold, and damp woman.

She was still beautiful.

He stepped out, expecting her to follow, but instead, she entered the elevator and pressed a button.

"Where are you going?" Charles tilted his head to one side.

"To bed. It's been a long day," Grace replied.

No!

"But I was just coming down to see you," he complained; Admittedly, he'd sounded like a small child who was being sent to bed without dessert.

"I'm sorry. I'm sure I'll see you tomorrow."

The doors closed, leaving him standing there, staring at the space where she'd been.

Chapter Five

GRACE WOKE WITH A SPLITTING HEADACHE. Could've been from the alcohol or the nightmares, but it was wicked. She grumbled and pulled herself out of bed, stumbling into the bathroom.

She dug for a bottle of ibuprofen that was ever-present in her makeup case. She never left home without it.

Grace filled a cup with cold water and took three, wishing the effects didn't take so long to kick in. When she headed back to the bed, her cellphone rang.

Since she didn't recognize the number, normally she'd send the call to email.

However, she was hoping for a call back, so she hit the green accept button.

"Ms. Harrison?"

"Yes, this is Grace Harrison."

"This is Anne-Marie with *Shockside Players*. It's my pleasure to announce you've made it to first call back. We would appreciate if you could please meet at the theater at noon today. Thank you." The woman hung up, without giving Grace a chance to say anything more.

She sat there a moment, shock rolling over her.

I made the first cut.

Grace stepped into the small dining area of the hotel, expecting to see many happy faces; that callbacks had happened for many people.

Unfortunately, the opposite was true. Surly and heartbroken actors mixed it with the occasional normal hotel guest.

They must've gotten the 'you didn't make the cut' call.

She stayed quiet, feeling guilty, as she filled her plate with scrambled eggs, a cinnamon roll, and a banana, made a cup of coffee. It was best to go eat alone in her room.

When she got out of the elevator and down the hall, there was something lying on the floor in front of her door.

A single red rose.

The rest of the hallway was empty, so there was no spotting the culprit. No sign of anyone.

She didn't have a free hand to grab the flower; she struggled to open the door with what she already held. Once inside, she set her food and coffee down and returned to grab the rose.

Grace got a glass of water and broke the stem so it'd fit in the cup, then set it beside the TV. She stared at the rose as she finished her breakfast.

Where did it come from? Why was it there?

It was very disconcerting.

The first rose, last night, was odd enough.

Because it arrived at the restaurant, it could've come from anyone.

But to find another in front of my hotel room door?

She gasped.

Someone's been watching me, following me!"

She'd left the rose from the night before at her table in *Hell's Kitchen*. She didn't know where it'd come from and was ashamed to admit, she *hated* roses.

With a passion.

She continued to stare at the rose, recalling the summer she was eight years old.

Grace had developed a horrible case of heat exhaustion. The house they'd lived in on-base had no air conditioning or a way to cool down the house.

She could remember few details. She'd been only in her underwear alone in her room, with her mother bringing her a cold washcloth every so often.

Grace recalled the feeling of being utterly alone and had been scared of dying, as she could hear other children playing happily outside.

The worst detail; she could smell the neighbor's rose garden through the open window.

From then on, the smell of roses always filled her with fear and dread.

Now, a single rose was doing just that.

Fear was climbing up her spine.

Someone had been *following* her last night.

Someone knew where she was staying.

It made her throat close up.

She was in a large metropolis where she knew *no one*, and had no family to come looking for her if she never came back.

Grace had even lost contact with her best friend over the last few years.

She felt so alone.

The more she looked at the rose, the more panicked she became.

Finally, she stood and snatched up the offensive flower, dropping it in the trash where she didn't have to look at it anymore.

"If I can't see it, it's not there," she said to calm herself.

It was barely ten a.m., but she had to get out of her room for some fresh air. Grace grabbed her jacket, handbag, and cellphone then headed out the door.

The day before, she'd seen a small cafe inside the huge convention center and figured it'd be a good place to start.

She could get a mocha and wait for callbacks to begin.

"Did you make it too, then?" the barista asked.

"Um, Excuse me?" Grace asked; she'd been lost in her own thoughts.

"The play going on? Did you make it?"

"Oh, um, yes, I did. But how did you know I was with the theater?"

The girl smiled politely before replying. "You just look like an actress. Are you famous, too?"

She shook her head no, a little embarrassed that this teen thought she was famous. It made her smile, and she cleared the last of the lingering fear she'd still held onto until then. She took her mocha and headed towards the little tables off to the left.

Grace pulled her laptop from her bag. She had work to do. When she was deep into a charity project, like she was with this one, she got lost in her work.

"Why is our leading lady sitting out here all alone, rather in the theater?" She jumped and looked up into beautiful brown and golden eyes.

"Charles, is it?" She played coyly, smiling sweetly, and tucking her laptop away. "And what do you mean by 'leading lady'? I'm sure if I get a part they'll cast me as a bearded woman or the chicken lady. Oh! If I'm really lucky, I might get to play Olga, the Snake Charmer."

They both laughed and made their way into the theater.

"Most of you aren't used to such a quick turnaround on callbacks. I know the average theater production audition takes up to a month before they make the final decision. I hope I made it clear in my advertisement, I do things differently."

There was an eruption of chatter, and Jason tried to get the small crowd to calm.

Grace glanced around. There were less than a quarter of the people that'd been there just the day before.

That gave her a hint of hope; she just might land a small role in the production after all.

"We will make our final decisions tonight and will notify those chosen by noon tomorrow. We're on a tight schedule and will have this show ready to be on the road by May fifteenth. We have a lot to get through today, in a short amount of time. So let's start with our 'fathers.' All men over forty, please come up to the stage."

Grace watched over the next three hours, as they auditioned for the minor characters. Sometimes they'd called actors by name, sometimes by age groups.

She'd been on stage twice, reading for a few minor characters. She actually read the lines for Olga, the Snake Charmer, and cringed inwardly that this really could be the role they gave her.

Could she take a role that wasn't Maddie?

Not because I think I'm the right choice for the character, but how heartbreaking would it be to come to rehearsals every day and not *get to be the character my heart cries for?*

She shook her head and returned to her seat.

I can't think like that.

She'd be honored to play any role in the production.

She didn't get much of a chance to interact with Charles, as he spent almost the entire day on the stage. It was clear he was a shoo-in for the role of Louis. Rarely did anyone else read for the character.

There was no singing today. Apparently, they'd already made their decision on who could sing, and who couldn't, through the basic auditions the day before. That, she was grateful for.

In my current state, I don't think it'd be a very good performance.

The body count in the room got smaller and smaller.

Grace had already been there for hours, and they'd yet to have anyone read for Maddie.

I really wish I'd eaten more at breakfast.

They had taken no break for lunch; maybe since they'd started at noon, but her blood sugar was getting low and her spirit, even lower.

She was about to call it quits for the night. They probably needed nothing more from her, since she hadn't been called back on stage in over two hours.

She'd just pushed open the doors to exit the auditorium when they'd called her name.

"Grace H. Please join us on the stage."

Her heart skipped when she slowly turned to face the stage.

One foot forward, then the next. Grace had to remind herself; picking up her feet completely as she walked, avoiding shuffling them, which was usually what caused her to fall over her own feet.

She made it to the stage, and Charles met her with an outstretched hand, helping her up the last few steps.

Someone handed her a paper, a scene from the play. It was the awkward scene, where the two lovers get their very first moments alone, and it proves to be less romantic than they'd hoped and dreamed it would be.

"If you'll please take a seat on the bench and follow the basic prompts on the sheets you hold," someone encouraged.

They obeyed. They had placed a bench in the center of the stage.

They took each other's hand.

Grace felt so comfortable just holding his hand, like old friends. She tried to slip into Maddie, as Charles began.

"Well, isn't this something," he said, as Louis.

"Something, yes," she replied, speaking for Maddie; her voice displaying the disappointment Maddie was feeling.

They both looked away from each other in awkward silence, yet still holding hands, until Charles spoke the next line.

"Maybe we could..." Louis hinted at a kiss, their first kiss.

Grace already knew what was next in the story. She closed her eyes and leaned forward.

She was ready for what should happen; not afraid, because she was Maddie.

Grace felt his hand slip up to touch her cheek before it continued back to get lost in her long hair, his thumb wrapped around the underside of her ear.

She kept her eyes closed when his soft lips caressed her own. Shivers of anticipation shot down her spine.

Her body reacted before her brain could, and Grace reached for him, to pull him in closer, to deepen the kiss.

Maddie was lost in that moment.

It was Grace kissing Charles. She was fully enjoying it. Her eyes popped open, just as the room exploded with cheers and laughter.

"Everyone, meet our Louis and Maddie!" Jason boomed.

Chapter Six

THIS IS RIDICULOUS. Why can't I sleep?

Charles rolled over for what felt like the two hundredth time, unable to get comfortable. He'd never had a woman affect him like this. He'd been with many women, even at twenty-one. The perks of being a pop star.

He glanced at the clock and groaned. It was barely two a.m. He put an arm over his eyes and tried to fall asleep again.

Just after dawn, he gave up and crawled out of bed. He grabbed his workout clothes; the best thing for him would be to hit the fitness center.

With his headphones in, Charles pushed himself longer than his body was used to. He needed the burn, a hard workout, the pain to rack his body, to help ease the torment in his mind.

He moved from the weights to the treadmill and he ran fast, trying to force thoughts of this woman from his mind. It didn't work. Every song blaring in his ear somehow tied back to her.

Grace, what is it about you? No one's ever done this to me. Maybe I should just leave. Not do the play. Just walk away.

The song came to an abrupt stop, replaced with a ringtone.

He didn't slow, only pressed the 'accept' button and snapped his greeting.

"This is Chuck, what do you want?"

"Don't be short with me, *Charles*. You're the one that left me a cryptic message."

"Oh, shit. Sorry, Jason. I didn't look to see who was calling. I'm in the gym." He decelerated the treadmill and came to a stop. "Thanks for getting back to me. My apologies about last night."

"What was that all about?" The director sounded more intrigued then irritated.

Charles grabbed a small towel off the rack by the door and wiped the sweat running down his face. He was overheated for sure, but only part of that was from the workout. He jumped back to his wants from the night before. "I told you when I signed on to do your little show; I needed to make sure my costar and I had chemistry, right?"

"What are you getting at, Charles? I haven't even started callbacks yet. So you can't complain about my choice for Maddie when I don't even know yet."

He pushed open the gym door and made his way to the stairs. What was the point of taking the elevator in a three-story hotel, right after a workout? "You've got it all wrong, Jason. You might not know, but I do. The moment I met her, I knew I'd found my Maddie." He sprinted up the three flights of stairs, feeling elated.

It didn't last long.

Jason retorted, his voice harsh. "Boy, you might be the name that'll get people to look our way, but you have no sway in who I pick for my leading lady. Your agent said you wouldn't be difficult. You've gone too far."

Charles kept his anger in check and was proud of himself. Normally, he'd explode at the man, but in the second of a heartbeat, he held his tongue.

If he screwed this up, he might never see Grace again.

They'd never have a chance encounter again, another opportunity to work together.

He took a deep breath. "You're right, and I'm not trying to throw my weight around. I just know what I saw last night; what I felt. This girl *is* your diamond in the rough. I don't think she even knows what talent she has. She embraced Maddie last night. She completely *became* her. I think you'd be a fool to let this one go." Charles reached his floor and opened the door. "Just watch her today and you will see. She *is* your Maddie." He disconnected the call, not letting Jason say another word.

He'd been hasty.

Shit!

He hadn't told Jason the name of the actress he was so passionate about.

Charles checked his fitness watch. He still had a few hours before callbacks, and he needed a shower.

Movement caught his eye. Grace exited the room and headed the opposite direction, toward the elevator.

He let her go, even though he didn't want to. He was fresh from a workout, and sweaty. Overheated. As soon as he heard the elevator *ding*, he hurried down the hall to see her room number.

He rushed back to his room and grabbed one of the roses he'd purchased the night before.

With great care, he put the rose in front of her door, leaving a token of his affection behind.

He went back to his own room and enjoyed his much-needed hot shower.

❦

BY THE TIME HE WAS CLEANED AND DRESSED, THE HOTEL WAS no longer serving breakfast. Not that he wanted any of the processed, unhealthily foods they offered. The only thing they had he would eat, was the bananas. Unfortunately, they were overly ripe and bruised.

"Coffee. I need coffee," Charles complained to himself.

He left the hotel and headed to his left. *Cafe Patteen* was just a few blocks away; he'd discovered it during his evening walk.

Why am I arguing with myself over coffee when I'm wide awake? To keep my thoughts off her. Yeah, good luck with that one.

For once he was grateful it took a lifetime to get through the line to get his much-needed caffeine. The chatter of the people in the line around him kept his mind off what he wanted to think most about.

It was nearly 11 a.m. by the time he got his organic coffee and yogurt parfait. He sat at one of the few small high top tables available, just long enough to eat his breakfast before heading over to the theater. He needed to catch Jason and clarify which actress he'd spoken of.

"Oh, shit!" Charles exclaimed aloud, causing a few passersby to glance his way as he rushed out of the café.

I don't even know if she made it to callbacks. She had to! There's no way he didn't pick her.

He quickened his step toward the theater. He had to get there before they started. If Grace hadn't made it to round two, *he* wouldn't go any further. Jason would need to find a new leading man.

Charles pulled open the glass door of the convention center with more force than necessary, feeling the protest in his sore muscles. He wanted desperately to call Jason again; give him more information, but had a feeling that doing so would push the man in all the wrong ways. He needed things to work in his favor.

As long as Grace had made it to callbacks, he could move things along, subtlety, not really letting the director see he was manipulating things to get his way.

The convention center interior seemed to go on for miles. He was in such a rush, he almost missed seeing the beautiful woman sitting at a small metal table, slowing drinking coffee, with her eyes locked onto her computer screen.

He stopped for a moment to silently observe her. Whatever she was working on, Grace was deep into. He smiled when she bit her at her ruby red lower lip, followed by pressing them together.

"Why is our leading lady sitting out here all alone, rather in the theater?"

When she looked up at him, her eyes sparkled green.

His breath caught in his throat at her smile.

"Charles, is it?" She looked away to place her laptop in the bag beside her. "And what do you mean by 'leading lady?' I'm sure if I get a part they'll cast me as a bearded woman or the chicken lady. Oh! If I am really lucky, I might get to play Olga, the Snake Charmer."

Thank God, she made it to first call back. I can make this work!

Charles laughed, offering her his arm to accompany her to the theater.

WHILE JASON GAVE HIS SPEECH ABOUT A QUICK TURNAROUND IN his theater company, Charles dared a glimpse at Grace. He couldn't have asked for a better scenario. He'd have Grace as his Maddie, wrapped in his arms within the week.

"We'll make our final decisions tonight and will notify those chosen by noon tomorrow. We're on a tight schedule and will have this show ready to be on the road by May fifteenth. We have a lot to get through today in a short amount of time. So let's start with our 'fathers.' All men over 40 please come up to the stage."

Charles was on and off the stage more this day than the previous. He didn't have time to pull Jason aside and discuss his thoughts on who the leading lady would be.

More than once, they called Grace on stage, each time to read for a minor role, never for Maddie.

This irritated him.

How is Jason going to see that she's the perfect Maddie if he doesn't give her the chance?

They were clearly starting to wind down for the night when he finally got a moment with Jason.

"About my leading lady..." Charles said.

"I know. You asked that she goes last. So she's going last."

"When did I..."

"Yesterday you asked for Grace to go last. After how you two were during the musical aspects of the audition, I assumed she's the lady you spoke of. So I saved the best for last. Right?"

He could only nod as the director stepped away to call her forward.

Charles watched as Grace slowly made her way to the stage, and he met her at the steps. He offered his hand and felt that spark return when they touched.

They were both given a sheet of paper, but he didn't bother to look at it.

"If you'll please take a seat on the bench, and follow the basic prompts on the sheets you hold," someone dictated.

Charles finally looked down at the paper, trying to fill his head with the dialogue and direction. It was hard, with Grace sitting beside him, her sweet smell filling his senses. He took her hand, grateful for the chance to touch her again, as he spoke his lines.

In the role of their characters, they looked away from each other for a moment of awkward silence.

Charles turned back to her, his voice full of the same apprehension Louis must feel.

The wanting. The desire. The need.

"Maybe we could..." Louis hinted at a kiss. Charles was trying to hold back his own excitement at what would essentially be *their* first kiss, too.

Grace, or Maddie, nodded.

Without hesitation, he reached for her; his hand caressing her cheek before he continued further back to let his fingers get lost in her long chestnut hair. It felt like heaven.

She closed her eyes.

He held his breath as he leaned in closer, building the anticipation.

This would be a kiss he hoped they *both* would remember for the rest of their lives.

Her soft lips were welcoming, just slightly parted. He brushed his lower lip with a feather-like touch across her upper lip.

Stage kissing differed slightly from kissing with a purpose, not quite full contact. There was no denying the passion in their kiss, even if it *was* a stage kiss.

Charles felt... sensed... when Maddie left and Grace took over.

Her hand touched the nape of his neck, pulling him in closer, to deepen the kiss, her body moving closer to his.

So close he could feel the heat radiating from her before she broke the kiss.

His body reacted, showing in great detail how she affected him.

He tried not to think of the strain on his jeans as the room exploded with cheers and laughter, and Jason's booming voice.

"Everyone, Meet our Louis and Maddie!"

Chapter Seven

"EXCUSE ME?"

Grace wasn't sure she'd heard correctly. She was still wrapped up in Charles, physically and emotionally. Her cheeks flushed and her lips were slightly bruised from the kiss.

She dropped her hand from his neck and tried to face whoever'd made the announcement, hoping her embarrassment wasn't written all over her face.

Charles reluctantly took his hand from her hair but moved it to her upper thigh.

She should shove him away—she didn't know this man, but he was helping keep her grounded.

"Did I... did I hear you right? *I'm* Maddie?" Her voice shook from the excitement and confusion. She was too old to play Maddie, by ten years easily.

"Don't you want the lead role?" Jason, the director, asked. He stepped closer to them on center stage, his voice low but his bright, his white smile gleaming.

"Yes! But..."

"No buts. Charles was right. You are the one." He whirled toward the rest of the production. "That's a wrap for tonight!

We'll be contacting everyone else that landed a role by noon, with instructions for where to meet tomorrow afternoon."

Grace looked at Charles.

He was beaming.

She was still in shock.

How did this happen? I only auditioned with one scene.

How had that been enough for Jason to make such an important decision?

"Get outta here, people! We're done for the night! Get some sleep. Some of you have a very busy day tomorrow and need all the rest you can get!"

Grace and Charles sat there a moment longer.

She couldn't move for fear if she did, the spell would break. *This* was a dream, a lifelong dream, being *handed* to her, and she was afraid it would disappear.

"Grace." Her new costar's voice broke through the fog.

She snapped her eyes to his face.

"I'm starving and would love to celebrate. Would you join me for dinner?" he asked.

Just then, like clockwork, her stomach rumbled.

"I'll take that as a yes," he teased.

She could only smile, fully embarrassed. She wanted to stand, but his hand still rested on her thigh, keeping her from going further.

"Give me just a moment. Let's wait for the theater to clear. I know the perfect place to go eat, but I don't want half the people here to follow us. You and I need some alone time."

Grace cocked her head to the side, curious about his choice of words.

"Well, think about it. We're gonna be playing love interests. Don't you think we should get to know one another a little better before we jump into such... intimate positions that these roles will put us in?"

She nodded. He was right but wished he'd chosen a better set of words for their upcoming situation. *'Intimate'* was one word she needed removed quickly.

Grace had to change the subject. "So, where are you taking me to eat?"

A short time later, they were sitting in the upper level of a small restaurant, located a few blocks from the convention center.

The place was styled after a British pub, complete with Manchester United and Chelsea Football Club banners on the walls.

Grace sat in awkward silence, waiting for the waiter.

What am I supposed to talk about with him?

They'd just had a rather passionate kiss.

I know he felt the heat I had, I could see it.

"WELCOME TO BRITT'S. WHAT CAN I GET YOU TWO TO DRINK? Our bottled beers are on the list there and I can tell you what's on tap."

Charles picked up the plastic frame that held the beer list and quickly chose one before handing it over.

"Do you have any hard ciders?" Grace asked.

"Oh, yeah. You should try this one." He pointed to a name on the list.

"Sounds good, thank you."

"Are you ready to order, or do you need another minute?"

She knew without looking at the menu what she wanted. Any time she went to a pub, Irish, British, or otherwise, she always ordered the fish and chips.

"Yeah, I'm ready. Are you?" he asked.

They both ordered and the waiter disappeared.

"So what made you pick this place?" Grace asked.

"Oh, I.. uh..." His cheeks brightened an adorable red.

His blush really showed his youthfulness.

"I saw it last night, after auditions. I went for a much-needed walk. I had to cool down. There were just too many actors at auditions that set off my temper. Seriously, if you're going to audition for a well-known traveling theater company, at least do your research and come prepared."

Heat flushed *her* face. She hadn't looked up *Shockside Players*. Grace hadn't cared. It was a chance to go on a little adventure without making a life-changing decision.

If she got a role, she'd still keep her home in Denver, but get the opportunity to do something different with her life. She wanted to branch out but wasn't ready to pack up her little apartment and leave the last state her parents had been alive in.

"Oh, I didn't mean you," Charles said.

"Huh?"

"You were blushing. I assumed you thought I meant you. I didn't. You at least had on the right kind of shoes and knew the production well. Probably better than Jason does."

Right then the waiter saved her by returning with their drinks.

She quickly brought the cold bubbly beverage to her lips and drank deep. The sweet, yet tart, flavor exploded on her tongue. She let out a sigh as she set the now half-empty bottle back on the table.

Charles had a huge grin on his face. "That good, huh," he teased.

"Yeah, it really is. Plus, it's the last night I'll have any alcohol until the show ends, so I really have to enjoy every drop."

"Seriously? No alcohol at all? For, what, five months?" His voice was full of concern and disbelief.

"None. Once I take on a role, I refrain from many things, liquor being just one."

"I'm afraid to ask what the other things are."

Grace smiled politely as she picked her drink back up and took another long pull.

How could she tell him something so personal?

She looked at him, *really* looked, taking in everything again. Not just his outward appearance, but everything about him.

Yes, he was very good-looking, and a great kisser. However, he was eight years younger. Very cocky. He acted like an only child, used to always getting his way.

She'd be spending the next four or five months with this man, this *boy*. They'd be placed in such intimate situations, like lovers.

They'd have to kiss every day. Not that it was a bad thing. He was a wonderful kisser. Grace could feel a primal attraction to him. Her body called out for his.

Her mind knew better.

So did her heart.

Can I really do this? Can I kiss him again and not lose my sanity?

"Grace," Charles prompted. "Where did you go just now?"

Her cheeks flushed hot again, making her want another sip of cider to give her a moment to collect herself. She was drinking it too fast and could feel it. "Oh, just thinking about what you asked. What else I give up."

"And?"

Before she could answer, the waiter brought their food out.

"Is there anything else I can get you?"

"Can I please get some malt vinegar and more lemons?" Grace asked.

"And she'll have another cider. Can you also bring a shot of Fireball?" Charles said.

"Of course. I'll have those right out."

"I really shouldn't have another one," she said once the waiter was far enough away.

"If it's your last night to drink, you really gotta enjoy it."

"I am enjoying it, Charles. I don't need more."

He wouldn't take no for an answer, encouraging her to finish the bottle she had while it was still ice cold.

When the waiter returned, her costar added the Fireball shot to her cider, prompting her to stick her thumb in the top and gently give the bottle a tip over, to mix the shot in. "Give that a try."

She hesitantly took a sip and was amazed at the assault on her taste buds. It was delicious, like nothing she'd tasted before.

No longer just sweet and tangy, it was also spicy. Grace had to be careful as she could easily down the drink, which wouldn't be good.

She had no problem with bottled drinks, but hard liquor always hit her differently... harder.

She picked at her fries as Charles spoke.

"So, Gracie, you were just about to tell me what other things you give up during a show." His voice was soothing and seductive.

"I was?"

"You were."

"Did you call me 'Gracie'?" The liquor was hitting her harder than normal.

Damn, I really should've eaten more at breakfast.

"Is that okay?"

"Um, yeah. Only my best friend, Hope, calls me Gracie. But I haven't seen her in a while. So, sure. You can call me that." She tried to shake her head clear. Why had she let him talk her into that second drink with the Fireball?

If it hadn't had the extra shot, she would've been fine. Between little food she'd eaten that day, and her heightened emotional state, it was getting the best of her.

She needed to stay focused.

"Quit changing the subject. What else do you give up?" Charles said, just short of a demand.

He would not let up, so she'd just give it to him straight.

"Well, no alcohol. No fried foods. Little to no soda. And... no relationships." She said each one with finality and she counted them on one hand. Grace looked up at him on the last words, staring deep into his brown eyes, making sure he was listening.

He was dangerous, to her body, her heart. That kiss she could easily make her fall for this cute costar.

She'd once sworn to never love again.

Grace could live vicariously through the roles she played, without letting someone into her life.

That was all the love she needed.

His face fell. "How can you have no relationships? Life is full of them."

"Well, I'm okay with friendship. Sometimes that's all you need in life. Someone you can call on, someone you can cry to, complain at. Intimate relationships are bad for a production. When costars have feelings for each other, it reflects in their performance. And believe me, I've seen some good shows tank because of off-stage relationships. No, thank you. I'll pass." Grace polished off the last of her cider. She wanted another, but she really should have a glass of water.

She finished the last of her fish and Charles waved the waiter over.

"Can I have our check, please?" he asked the man.

His eyes pinned her in her seat, as soon as the man was away from their table.

"I really need to get you into bed."

Grace's breath evaporated.

Chapter Eight

"WHAT DID YOU SAY?" Grace blurted, her cheeks a bright crimson.

"You're tipsy, and we have a long day tomorrow. I should get you back to the hotel safe." His choice of words almost screwed everything. Sure, he wanted to get her into bed, naked and pressed against his body.

She'd made it perfectly clear that wasn't about to happen.

Not right away.

He'd have to work her over, and not in the way he really wanted to.

"Yeah, I think I should've just had one cider. My head is a little... dizzy. And we have a long day tomorrow."

The waiter returned and before Grace could grab the bill, Charles slipped the waiter eighty dollars and told him to keep the change.

He just wanted to get Grace out of there.

Charles jumped up and slid her chair out, allowing her to stand. Once they stepped outside, he slipped his arm around her, resting on her shoulders. He was grateful when she didn't protest or move away.

She fit perfectly against his body.

He couldn't let this go.

They walked in silence, just enjoying the sounds of the night. There was no one else on the street, except for the occasional car. He had so many things he wanted to say, needed to ask, and she was inebriated so, he hoped this was the right time. He wasn't taking advantage of her. So he told himself.

But what to start with?

"So, ah, Grace. If you won't do a relationship while doing a show, does that mean you'll be breaking some poor guy's heart tomorrow?"

She smiled, her cheeks were red from the alcohol.

Or maybe the question?

"Nah. I've been single for a while. It's just me and my plants."

Good. No one to interfere.

"You at least keep in touch with friends, family, right?"

"Nope. Don't have any."

He arched an eyebrow. Surely she was saying those things because she was drunk, not because it was true. "Damn, you're a cheap date. I've never had a girl get this drunk on me before."

Grace stopped walking, slipped his arm off her shoulder, and whirled to face him, placing her warm hands on his chest. "I'm not a cheap date. I didn't have lunch! And we're *not* on a date!"

Rather than snapping back—which was his normal response when someone yelled at him, he flashed his million-watt smile. Putting his hands over hers, Charles could keep her close. "I meant no disrespect. I just can't see how a woman as beautiful and talented as you would choose to have no friends."

"I have friends," she barked. Grace pushed off him, breaking their contact, and started walking away. "I just don't talk to them often. I'm too busy. Theater life and all."

It sounded like excuses. There was something underlying in there. Something he was determined to find out.

Maybe not tonight, but soon.

"Everyone needs someone to talk to. I at least have my older brother, even if we don't always get along. I know I can call him. Do you have someone?"

She stopped, her head tilted up at the tall building beside their hotel like she was contemplating something grand. It took much longer than it should have for her to answer; it made his heart beat a little faster.

Could things really be that simple for him?

That easy to slip into her life?

"I have Hope. We talk on the phone... sometimes. Maybe once a month, or every two months. I can't remember." She sighed. "I really miss my friend."

Yeah, she's drunk.

Charles slipped his arm back around her shoulders, pulling her close to him. They were right in front of their hotel, but she hadn't seemed to notice. "Gracie. We're gonna be real good friends. Would that be all right with you, if I be your friend? You can call on me if you need someone to talk to. My twin sister says I'm a very good listener."

She looked his way, but her eyes didn't really focus on his face. "You have siblings? I thought you were an only child."

He tried not to laugh. "Yeah, I have a few. My twin sister, Angel and I, are the youngest, then there's Barbara, Lisa, and the oldest is Nick."

"Wow. I'm jealous. I never had siblings. Just Mom and Dad. Until they were gone. And Hope. Sometimes I have Hope. I wish we weren't too busy all the time. I miss her."

She was cute when she was drunk. She kept repeating herself, but it didn't bother him. His heart melted when she smiled, her eyes closing slowly, then opening ever so slightly.

"I like you, Charles."

His heart slammed against his ribs; his stomach tightened.

"You can be my friend. I think you'll be a good friend."

Her hooded eyes were seducing him, whether or not she meant to. Her rosy lips were beckoning.

Grace blinked slow and sexy again, and when her eyes shut, Charles leaned down and took possession of her lips.

❦

HIS LIPS WERE WARM AND INVITING, TEASING HERS TO DANCE with him.

Grace gave in, not thinking about, well... anything; just enjoying the sweet taste of him.

His arms snaked around her, taking full control of the situation, their bodies melting together, fitting perfectly.

His fingers found their way to the nape of her neck, into her hair, gripping with the right amount of pressure, giving her a thrill she'd never experienced.

Her heart raced, adrenaline pumping through her veins along with the alcohol, fueling her in a way she'd never known.

She couldn't breathe.

Grace had to break away and catch her breath.

Charles relaxed his hold on her, sliding his hand down her arm to grab her hand. Without speaking a word, he pulled her along, entering the hotel and rushing to the elevator. He pressed the second-floor button and as the doors closed; he pulled her back into his arms.

She lost not only her breath but her mind at that moment.

He knew what he was doing; his mouth was made of magic.

The elevator door opened, and they giggled like children when he dragged them down the hallway to her room.

Grace couldn't get her key out of her back pocket, her hands weren't working like they should.

"Let me help you," he whispered in her ear.

Goosebumps erupted up into her hairline. She handed him the keycard, and the door opened. She stepped in and the cold air-conditioned breeze hit her with a chilling blast, cooling not only her cheeks but her lust.

Charles stepped up behind her and moved her hair to rest on one shoulder so he could begin raining kisses on her neck. He pressed his body close to hers, so close she could feel his erection against her hip.

Like a bucket of ice water, reality came crashing down.

She was about to ruin everything she'd built up, worked hard for.

Grace faced Charles, anger now fueling her.

"You need to get the hell out of here!" She pushed at his chest.

"Grace?"

"No! Get out!" She reached around him to open the door, expecting him to be the gentleman and just leave. "You're trying to take advantage of me!"

Charles had encouraged all the alcohol, even when she'd voiced her reservations. He'd just wanted to get down her pants!

She wasn't that kind of girl!

Instead, he reached for her, cupping her cheek and leaning in to kiss her again. "Just one kiss," he whispered against her lips.

How had he gotten so close?

"No. Charles, leave now." Her voice hid the shaking her body was doing.

He turned and walked out, not saying a word as the door closed behind him.

Shock rolled over her.

Grace rushed to the bathroom and splashed cold water on her face, then put her wet hands on the back of her neck, trying to cool down further.

How could she have let things go that far? She'd acted like some hormone-raging teen. *Nothing* like her rational self.

How can he affect me like that?

She had sworn off love years ago; she'd never love another, in any shape or form. Taking on characters' love lives for a short period of was all she needed.

That and the occasional romance novel.

They were safe.

They didn't cause unnecessary pain.

Had the careless kisses she'd just shared with Charles, ruined her chance of a lifetime?

What do you think you were doing?

Her head was still fuzzy, despite the rude awakening.

Not only is he eight years younger, I can't *let anyone into my heart.*

Never again.

She quickly undressed, then turned on the shower, not waiting for it to get warm.

It didn't matter if it was cold or not. The water helped wash away her emotions and her fears.

Grace crawled into bed, pulling the covers up to her chin, cocooning herself in the blankets.

She'd have to confront Charles in the morning.

We can't start a show like this. I've dreamed of playing this role since I was a child. I can't screw this up!

She fell asleep with his scent still lingering in the room.

❧

CHARLES OPENED HIS DOOR, SET THE KEYCARD ON THE nightstand and looked at the roses sitting in a beer bottle on the desk.

The sweet aroma of the flowers filling his room still made him think of Grace.

Her lips had been rose-red, and as soft as a petal. She'd opened up to him, much like a bud in bloom.

Then shut him down the moment things got hot.

What the hell?

He would not give up.

She'd said she gave up relationships, but she can't really mean it.

The anger in her voice had said she was serious. At least when it came to intimate relationships.

With three sisters, Charles had become very good at being the 'friend' to many a girl. His sisters' friends had come to him for advice on boys, or a shoulder to cry on. They usually left with a smile on their faces, and it wasn't simply because he listened.

He sat at the desk, continuing to stare at the roses. What he wanted was a shock, but he couldn't follow through. Yet. He glanced at the clock. Had enough time had passed?

After waiting almost forty-five minutes, Charles stood, reached for a stem, and headed out the door; Grace's room key in his other hand.

He held his breath as he slowly opened her door.

The room was dark, but the light from the hallway still illuminated her.

Charles stepped into the room and quietly shut the door, waiting for a response from his Sleeping Beauty.

Nothing happened.

She was deep asleep, her breathing soft and soothing.

He could stay there all night, just looking at her.

They had a long day ahead of them, and he needed sleep.

Charles crept up to the edge of her bed, taking her into his lungs and holding it there. He reached across her to place the single red rose on the pillow beside her, so when she woke, it would be the first thing she saw.

He set her room key on the nightstand, close to her purse and with great care, then slipped out the door.

Chapter Nine

GRACE WOKE with a yawn but stopped mid-breath. Her senses were overwhelmed with the smell of roses. Her eyes flew open to find a single rose, inches from her face.

Her heart slammed against her ribs. She flew off the bed, panic flying up to her throat, strangling, making her choke.

Fear froze her against the door to the room, but her eyes were glued to the offensive item in on her pillow.

What the hell?

Breaking her eyes away, she scanned the room for any other signs there'd been an intruder.

Her purse was right where she left it, her room key beside her phone. Her clothes were still in a heap on the floor by the bathroom. Nothing looked amiss, other than the damned flower in her bed.

Her hand went to her neck. She tried to calm her racing heart. Who could have done this?

How did they get in?

Grace rushed to the phone, pressing the option for the front desk.

"Perry speaking, how may I help you?"

She swallowed once, then again, her throat dry from her fear. "I... uh... someone came into my room last night, while I was sleeping."

"Ms.... um, Harrison. Are you all right?" He didn't sound concerned.

"I'm fine. It's just... they left a rose on my pillow."

The line was silent for a moment.

"Sounds sweet. You must have a secret admirer."

His words send angry heat spiraling up her spine.

"Are you kidding me? I tell you someone entered my room while I was sleeping and you say, 'sweet'? I want your manager! I want to know who was in my room!" Her knuckles whitened, and the phone creaked from her tight grip.

"One moment, please."

The line clicked and terrible elevator music blasted in her ear.

Grace looked over at the red bud and tried to calm herself enough to replay the night's events.

She'd had dinner with her new costar...

Charles. Could he have done this?

She looked at her key on the nightstand and shook her head. He'd brought her to her room; they'd been kissing.

He'd wanted more.

She'd pushed him out of her room and he'd left without another word. Her key was right where she'd left it.

Hadn't she left it there?

She couldn't actually remember setting the key down, that much was still unclear.

"Miss?"

The voice on the line snagged her attention.

"I'm so sorry there was a miscommunication with our new front desk clerk. If I understand right, you think someone entered your room without your permission?"

"Correct."

"Unfortunately, there's no way for us to investigate this. The keycards are not traceable. But I'd like to comp your stay with us and move you to another room. I suggest you utilize the locking mechanism at the top of the door for your additional safety."

Grace didn't know what to say.

Really, what had she expected?

Cameras in the hallways? Not at a mid-level hotel like this.

She accepted the comp and the offer of a new room. She packed up in record time, and left the damned rose on the bed, slamming the door behind her.

※ ✿

THWAP, THWAP, THWAP.

Charles slammed the red dodge ball on the hardwood floor of the community center's recreation room like a basketball. He was irritated; with himself, with Grace.

He'd thought things had gone well last night.

Until Grace had shoved him out of her room, right when things were getting good.

I've never had a woman deny me before. What the fuck's up with that?

Yes, she'd been drunk, and he took things too far. He'd left her a rose, his way of apologizing if he'd pushed things too far. Had she accepted it?

Rehearsals were supposed to start almost an hour ago, and she still wasn't there.

He slammed the ball down again. He looked up when it returned to him, and all the anger disappeared.

A vision of beauty stood before him.

Her long hair was pulled back into a ponytail and her cheeks were flushed pink. The buttons of her light green shirt were slightly askew.

She must've been in a hurry to return to me.

Relief flooded through him when she came closer.

"Gracie! You're here! It's about damn time! We can't get started without you. Hey! Catch!" Charles playfully threw the ball at her.

She stepped out of the way before it could collide with her. The flying red rubber hit the wall behind her only to roll back their way.

"Seriously, Grace. Would it really hurt that much if it hit you?" Charles crossed his bare arms over his chest, trying to fake disappointment.

"Everyone please take your seats, I don't care where. Just sit and I'll pass out the scripts," Jason said.

Charles led his beautiful costar to the ring of chairs, indicating she should sit right beside him. He did his best not to laugh while she rolled and unrolled her script.

Something was on her mind, something that caused her cheeks to lose their color.

Did I do this to her?

He bumped her shoulder, trying to get her attention. "Are you ready for your life to change?" he whispered in her ear.

She glanced his way, fear written all over her beautiful face. Her brows furrowed, and she swallowed. "Did you come into my room last night?" Her voice waved slightly.

"You know I did." He wagged his brows at her.

"I'm serious, Charles," she whispered, but spared a glimpse to Jason, who was engaged in a discussion with the two men chosen to play their characters' fathers.

"Is this about the kiss?" He asked, but didn't mention his little gift.

She shook her head. "Someone came into my room when I was sleeping."

He could hear real fear in her voice.

"There was a rose on my bed. And it wasn't the first left for me. Someone's been following me, and I'm scared."

Oh shit, what have I done?

Jason asked everyone to open their scripts, and they began their first reading.

Two hours later, they'd finished with a full read-through.

Charles always loved the first meeting of a new show and getting to hear how people changed their voices and body language when pretending to be someone else. Even Grace was different.

COLOR HAD FLOODED HER CHEEK, SHE SAT A LITTLE straighter, even her laughter was lighter.

She really transformed into her character.

This will be a damn good show, if I don't screw things up.

Jason thanked everyone for coming and handed out the actors' information packet.

"We're doing things differently than any other production before. This show is unlike any I've done in the past. It'll be treated as thus. I have a large ranch out in Montana; we'll stay the first three weeks. There're two bunker houses where you'll be living, guys in one, girls in the other. I will have *no* consorting during rehearsals or production. Is that clear?" Jason looked right at Charles.

He looked down at the packet and thumbed through it absentmindedly, ignoring the words clearly pointed at him.

Screw you, Jason.

He'd bide his time.

Grace already made it known she'd have nothing to do with him until the show was over, at least not romantically.

In the meantime, he'd do what he did best.

Woo her secretly.

He'd get under her skin in all the right ways; convince her he was her best friend. Having sisters had taught him a lot, like patience and how to listen. Every girl needed a guy best friend. "You have one week to get your affairs in order and get to the ranch. All talent *must* arrive by Tuesday next week. You can come as early as Monday, but anyone that hasn't checked in to the ranch by nine p.m. on Tuesday will lose their position in the production. I'm taking this show to a new level and will *not* accept less than the best. Is this understood?"

The crowd made it known, and Jason released them.

The actors began filing out of the rec room, a buzz of excitement around them.

Including Grace.

Charles offered a hand to his beautiful costar, helping her out of her seat.

"Do you have any plans tonight?" he asked with a hint of anticipation. He was proud he'd been able to keep it from his voice.

"Actually, I think I should head home. I could get at least a few hours of drive time in. It would get me to Denver faster."

No, I can't let her leave yet!

"Grace, it's really not a good idea for you to drive this late at night. You've had a long day. I'm sure your hotel will still charge you for the room since you didn't check out by eleven. Why don't we have dinner tonight, I promise I'll be a gentleman? You can get a good night's sleep, and head out first thing in the morning."

She stopped walking, causing Charles to do the same. The color in her cheeks from moments before had paled. "Technically, my room's free tonight. The hotel's trying to make up for... well, something that happened last night. I'm ready to go home. Honestly, I'm scared to spend another night in that hotel."

"Why? Because of our kiss last night? I promise it won't happen again."

She sighed. "Someone's been leaving me roses, I'm deathly afraid of roses. It's just set me off-kilter. I'm really excited to be doing the show but I cannot *wait* to get out of Minneapolis." There was a hint of a quiver in her voice.

They reached the door to the front of the building and he held it open for her.

The evening was once again chilled, and she wrapped her arms around herself to keep the cold wind off her bare skin. She was wearing short sleeves.

"Let's go have dinner, and you can tell me all about these roses."

Chapter Ten

GRACE SIPPED WATER while they waited for their food to arrive, wishing she hadn't made a pact with herself to give up certain things. The first read-through of a role was the beginning of her celibacy.

Tonight she could really use a drink. Even if it was just the bubbly carbonation of an ice-cold soda. The boring clear fluid would have to do.

She set her glass down and continued to explain her dilemma. "First there was the rose at the restaurant, then the one outside my door, then in my hotel room. Seriously, how could someone gain access to my hotel room? It had to be through housekeeping. They must've gotten someone to let them in." She watched her costar's face closely.

Could it have been Charles?

His expression showed no signs he was the culprit.

"Not to sound insensitive, but you weren't hurt. Just spooked. Is it worth continuing to stress over?" He picked up his beer and downed the entire contents in just a few gulps.

"I'm scared. That's not something to take lightly. My fear is real. Don't discount that."

Charles reached across the table and took her hand, running the pad of his thumb across her knuckles in a comforting gesture. "I'm sorry, that wasn't my intention. I'm simply stating it's not good to continue to worry about it. I get it, you're afraid. You have every right to be. But you don't have to face this alone. I don't think it's a good idea for you to drive home tonight, especially since you're scared. Your state of mind isn't in the right place. Why don't you stay with me—"

She put a hand up to stop him.

"I've got a room with double beds. Remember, I have sisters. I know how to be a gentleman. I apologize for my behavior last night. It was inappropriate. I spent the rest of the night thinking about what I did. I want this show to work. It will be the best show Shockside has ever done. And I think it's because of the chemistry you and I have."

Grace said nothing, letting him go on. She arched an eyebrow, but he didn't seem to react. Evidently, he didn't get her, *are you serious?* she was trying to project.

"We're about to spend the next four months together. I want you to know from the beginning you can trust me, come to me for anything. This is the best time to show that. I hope you never experience this type of fear again." His words were so sincere, the tone of his voice saying he truly meant the words he spoke.

Maybe he's right. I'm making a big deal out of this.

Grace took another sip of water, trying to find the right words. She didn't want to lead him on, but she could use a friend.

The waiter interrupted them, holding two plates in his hands. "Is there anything else I can get for you?" He asked after setting them down.

"I think we're good," Grace let him know.

"Are you excited about the ranch? I've never done a production like this. I'm apprehensive about living with the cast before we hit the road. There'll already be enough tension during the show. Have you ever done a traveling show before?"

Grace's face flushed hot. "I haven't. The shows I've done in Denver have all been in one theater or another. Stationary. So, yeah. I'm looking forward to it." She cut into her meat and busied herself with eating. It was difficult, not because the food wasn't enjoyable, she was always up for a good steak.

She had too much on her mind. Not to mention the knots in her stomach.

This was going to be a life-changer, but worry scattered her self-confidence. This could lead to so many things, including furthering her career as an actress.

That's what I need to focus on. Just that. Only that.

Being the best actor she could be.

Charles chatted about some of the other productions he'd done, and a bit about his family, but she was absentmindedly picking at her food, not really absorbing the information.

Once again, he took care of the bill before she had a chance to do anything about it.

They walked in silence the six blocks from the restaurant to the hotel. The hotel marque was just coming into sight when Charles let out a sigh and broke the silence.

"Seriously, though, Grace. You should come stay with me tonight. Just so you're not alone. If I prove to be anything less than a true gentleman, I give you permission to geld me."

Laughter rumbled in her belly as it carried up her body to release into the night air. "Well, that's a promise I've never been given. But, okay. You're right. I really don't want to be alone tonight. My things are all still packed in my suitcase from moving this morning. I just have to run to my new room and get them. It should give you time to pick up all your dirty underwear from off the floor."

This time, he laughed.

They entered the hotel, followed by the elevator. Charles pressed his floor and Grace had to hold back a laugh.

Sure it was a small hotel, but they were now on the same floor.

When the doors opened, she headed to the left, and he to the right.

"I'm in 227. See you in a few minutes!" he called over his shoulder.

She slid the keycard across the pad and entered her room

The cold of the air conditioner hit her.

Why do they always have the rooms so cold? It's warmer outside in the brisk April night.

Grace used the restroom, brushed her teeth, and did a basic bedtime prep, in case Charles was all nasty male and the bathroom was gross.

She took one last look in the mirror before heading out.

🌿🔥

CHARLES SMILED AS HE TOUCHED HIS KEYCARD TO THE LOCK. He had Grace right where he wanted her. When he opened the door, the smell of roses swept over him.

Oh shit! I gotta get those out of here!

He rushed over to the remaining flowers, still sitting in the last of the water. He scooped them up and whirled, not once, but twice.

What the hell was he supposed to do?

He opened the door, scanning to see if his costar had left her room yet.

The hallway was empty, thank God.

Charles looked both left and right, trying to assess his options. The stairs where just off to his left, as far away from Grace's new room as possible.

He dashed for the stairs and football-tossed the fully bloomed flowers over the railing. He didn't stay to watch them flutter to the landing below.

Back in the safety of his room, Charles threw open the window before he ran to the bathroom and grabbed his cologne.

He sprayed the heady *Tom Ford For Men* around the room, hoping the intense musk scent would mask the aroma of the roses.

He'd just set it back in the bathroom when he heard a gentle knock. He waved his arms to spread the smell and headed to the door to let her in.

The moment she stepped into the room, he knew she couldn't tell there had been roses in his room for days. She did, however, notice the overwhelming amount of cologne. Her nose wrinkled. "Um, Charles, if we're gonna make this work..."

He raised an eyebrow in anticipation of the things *he* wanted to work on.

She must've seen something in the way his body responded because her jaw flexed. Grace was about to set him straight. "Things as in, working together on this show, and being in a shared space; you will have to learn not to bathe in cologne. I promise, it doesn't make you more attractive. If anything, it turns people away. A little goes a long way. Can you remember that?"

All he could do was nod. He had to hide a smirk, too.

She most definitely had no clue *he* was the rose bearer.

He needed to keep it that way.

"The bed closest to the window is untouched if you'd like to take that one?" Charles offered, as she wheeled her suitcase to the open space by the wall, just in front of the fake walnut desk.

"Thank you."

He couldn't help but watch as she leaned over to open her bag and pull a few things out. His body responded to the curves of her backside, and he had to take a deep breath to get his body under control.

She slipped off into the bathroom with a small pile of clothing in her hands.

Pajamas, I'm guessing. Damn, too bad she doesn't sleep naked. Guess I better not.

He reached into his own suitcase to pull out a clean T-shirt and boxer briefs. He slipped into the fresh clothes right as Grace stepped out of the bathroom, shutting the light off as she emerged.

"I appreciate your hospitality, but like you pointed out, it's been a long day for me, and I have a lot of driving tomorrow. So please forgive me if I just curl up and pass out." She crossed over to the second bed, pulled back the covers and slipped in between the sheets.

Grace was asleep almost as soon as her head hit the pillow. The soft breathing and occasional delicate snores spoke of it.

She was comfortable with him.

Why else would she be able to fall asleep so fast?

Charles wasn't so lucky. He lay there for hours with just the small reading light connected to his headboard turned on. It was enough to illuminate his gorgeous costar.

He watched her turned over in her sleep.

She'd started out facing away from him, in the direction of the window, but had rolled and now faced him.

In the dim light, he could see the slight parting of her soft pink lips. Her long lashes rested on her high cheekbones.

A strand of her chestnut hair had fallen forward across her face. It took all his strength not to reach out and slip the piece back behind her ear.

He could lay there forever and just watch her sleep. However, he needed to get a little rest, too. Right as the sun was beginning to peek through the curtains, Charles drifted off to sleep.

Chapter Eleven

GRACE STRETCHED OUT, pulling all her muscles tight then relaxing. This bed wasn't any different from the previous room she'd been in, yet it seemed like she'd gotten much better sleep that night. She rubbed at the dust in the corners of her eyes and rolled over to glance at her roommate.

Charles was still passed out. He was curled up on his left side, facing her. A wisp of blond hair caressed his cheek, hiding one of his closed eyes. He looked like a young boy.

It reminded her he was just that; still a boy.

Their eight-year age difference would be one of the many things that helped her keep a promise; to never give herself to a man again. In any form. She could see herself becoming friends with him, though.

That much she could give him.

Grace quickly and quietly slipped from the bed, rustled through her suitcase to grab the things she'd need in the bathroom. She locked the door the moment she had it shut.

She wanted to take a quick shower and getting on the road. She just wanted to get back to Denver. Even if it was only for a few days.

She sighed when the warm water cascaded down her back. She was feeling good about everything. The creepy stalker and the roses were slipping into the furthest recesses of her mind.

In less than an hour, she could be on her way home, away from everything bad that'd happened the last forty-eight hours.

Within a week, her new life would be starting.

There were far too many good things ahead of her to focus on anything negative.

Find only the good in life, Elvis.

Her mother's words filled her mind.

Elvis.

Only her mom and Hope could call her that.

With the hot water soothing her body, the memory of her mother and her words of encouragement soothed her soul.

She couldn't recall when her mother had first called her 'Elvis', but it'd stemmed from the fact that her first and middle names said together quickly sounded like Elvis's mansion. Grace Lynne.

Grace chuckled to herself at the memory, as she wrapped a towel around her body.

Would there ever be a day she'd trust a man enough to allow him to call her such a special nickname?

She shook her head.

She'd given up on real love.

Fairytales and romance novels were the only places true love existed.

Grace wiped the condensation off the mirror with a clean washcloth she'd found on the counter. The woman in the reflection stared back at her. Bright blue-green eyes locking on themselves.

She ran her hands over her forehead and into her wet hair, causing the wispy chestnut strands in the front to stand on end. For just a moment, she saw the scared little girl in there; the girl that'd once been so bullied she'd become silent. Someone who couldn't make new friends.

Oh, how her life had changed.

The theater had changed her.

Now, she was going to change theater.

Grace was ten years older than the character she was about to portray.

Shockside Theater Troupe was taking a well-known, one-set show, and spinning it on its ear with all the new technology.

This *was* going to be a show like no other.

She was terrified she was going to screw everything up.

Charles is dangerous.

He was clearly used to having any girl he wanted.

He can't have me.

He was a charmer, and they always broke hearts. She'd never let that happen again.

She got dressed.

Grace needed to get on the road, not only because it was a fourteen-hour drive, but she had to get away from her new costar and the temptations he's oozed.

She pulled her hair back into a haphazard bun, put on just a swipe of mascara, gathered her things and headed out into the bedroom.

CHARLES WOKE WITH A START AS THE BATHROOM DOOR CLOSED and the lock slid over. He glanced at the empty bed.

He slipped out of his bed and moved over to hers; one of the unused pillows from his bed in his hands. He leaned down to inhale the pillow she'd slept on last night.

Her scent still lingered on the fabric.

He picked it up, putting the one from his bed in its place, pressing on the center to make it look like it'd been used during the night.

Charles returned to his bed, her pillow in his hands.

Slipping back under the covers, he held her pillow tight. His body reacted as her delicate fragrance filled his senses.

His cock hardened and trembled in anticipation of her hot, wet core tightening around him.

He closed his eyes and imagined how she must look in the shower, as his hand slipped under the covers.

Grace's creamy skin, wet from the hot water caressing her body, touching her in all the places he wished his hands were.

Charles pictured droplets of water trailing down the valley between her breasts as her pink nipples puckered. He envisioned every inch of her body.

He stroked faster, pretending it was her hands on him, doing all the things he liked done. He bit back a groan, not wanting her to hear him pleasuring himself.

Charles breathed in sharply between clenched teeth when his climax hit. It was coming too fast, too soon, but he couldn't stop it.

His seed filled his hand since he hadn't prepared with something to catch it. The shower shut off and he was in a rush to clean up the mess he'd made.

He glanced around the room. What could he do? Under the desk was a towel from the pool area he'd forgotten to pick up. He used it to clean himself, not worrying about the bed.

He'd be checking out soon. Charles tossed the towel back under the desk, careful not to let anything slip out.

He'd just pulled his clothing for the day from his suitcase when the door to the bathroom opened.

The heat and steam hit him just a moment before her scent did. He inhaled, filling his lungs with her, and couldn't help his sigh.

Why does she affect me like this?

This was something he desperately wanted to know the answer to, and someday he would know. However, not today.

Grace smiled as she stepped out. "The bathroom's all yours."

He could only nod, dancing around her to enter the over-heated room.

Charles worried she'd take off while he was in the bathroom, so he showered quickly, not even waiting for decent water temperature. *He couldn't let me leave without saying goodbye.*

He'd be seeing her again in less than a week, but he didn't want to lose any time with her.

He tried not to think about her being just where he now stood, in the same state; he'd already been there once in his mind.

Charles intentionally recalled the roses. They'd been meant as a loving gesture but had almost ruined everything. How was he to know she was deathly afraid of them and the scent they provided?

Weren't all women supposed to love roses?

Guess my Gracie isn't like other women.

He left the shower in record time and dressed, struggling to get his jeans on still-damp skin. He fought with his jeans, finally stopping to dry his legs thoroughly before resuming. He threw open the bathroom door with gusto.

Charles had been right, she was sneaking out.

Grace had just opened the door, her suitcase in one hand, a purse and laptop bag over the other shoulder. Her cheeks flushed pink, and even though it was adorable, she was embarrassed.

"What're you doing?" he blurted.

"Oh, I, um..." Her cheeks brightened more, and her eyes darted down to her suitcase then up at him. "I don't do goodbyes well. I was going to take my things to the car and grab a coffee from the lobby. I have a fourteen-hour drive, after all."

How could he be mad at her, after she'd shared something like that?

It felt personal. Like she cared enough about him already, it would be too hard to say goodbye.

He smiled so big he could feel the corners of his eyes crinkling. "Can I at least walk you to your car?"

She said nothing but nodded.

Moments later, they were standing next to her car, coffee in hand.

Grace slipped into the driver's seat and Charles leaned over, peering in at her.

"Safe driving. We can't have anything happen to our leading lady."

She grabbed the door handle and pulled at the door slowly. "I guess I'll see you in a week."

He stepped back so she could shut the door. "See you in a week," he whispered back.

She backed the car out, and his gaze followed her car until he could see it no longer.

"See you in my dreams tonight," Charles whispered aloud.

Chapter Twelve

ONE WEEK LATER, Charles was pacing outside the main cabin of the ranch where people were slowly trickling in as the sun was setting.

He'd been there since early that Monday morning. He'd taken a direct flight from Burbank, jumped in an Uber, and had been one of the first people to check into the ranch.

He watched as car after car filed in, not one holding Grace.

She technically didn't have to arrive for another day.

Charles was about to hunt down Jason and get her number to call and make sure she was okay when he saw her car coming down the dirt road.

The dust and dirt the green car was kicking up almost hid the make and model, but the dark blue-green color that closely matched her eyes, was unmistakable.

He was still grateful he'd been able to walk her to her car that morning in Minneapolis.

Otherwise, he wouldn't have known what her car looked like.

Charles was at her car, pulling open the door before she'd even put the car in park.

Her laughter filled his ears, as Grace unbuckled her seat belt and attempted to get out of the vehicle.

He tugged her into a tight hug. "I've missed you," he whispered.

"Um, hey. I, uh, can't breathe."

They both chuckled as he let her go.

"Shall we get you checked in?"

She nodded and grabbed her purse from the passenger seat.

A short time later, they entered the woman's bunker.

This was the only day they would allow the men to enter. After sundown that night, each bunker was gender-specific, unless otherwise noted.

Charles had learned they'd a few trans people in the show but didn't know who.

The building was broken down into four bedrooms. Each room had two sets of bunk beds, accommodating four women in each room.

They had given Grace room three; she'd be with the contortionists.

Jason had stated he hoped everyone would be comfortable with their roommates and would stick with the same actors once they began traveling. It just made things easier.

Charles glanced around the room. The women's rooms were identical to the men's. He was sharing a room with the two older men playing Louis and Maddie's fathers, and Victor—the man playing Der Hahn, the villain.

They all seemed to get along so far, but if things didn't go the way he wanted, a conversation with Jason would clear it all up.

He offered Grace his hand, after she tucked her suitcase under her bunk bed, and they headed for the main cabin.

Actors were scattered around, some munching on the buffet-style food laid out across a massive table, others mingling, getting to know the production team better.

"Have you eaten yet today?" he asked.

"It's been a few hours, and I wouldn't mind grabbing a bite."

They made their way to the table and filled their paper plates. However, when they went further into the large room, there didn't seem to be anywhere to sit.

"I think I saw some rocking chairs on the side of the house. Should we check there?" Grace said.

He smiled. What a lover-like thing to do, sitting on rocking chairs on the porch like an old married couple.

He let her lead the way. Sure enough, there were two empty chairs, just waiting for them.

Charles let her choose first, and he took the one not in direct sunlight. He wanted her to always feel like she came first.

The evening was beautiful. The ranch was laid out just right; their view from the front porch seemed to go on forever.

There were trees on either side, running down the length of the property. The sky was pink, orange and purple. Like a painting or on a postcard, only in real life.

He glanced at Grace.

She was observing the same sight, the richness of the night.

He gently brushed the tips of his fingers down the length of her arm, grabbing her attention. "I could stay here, like this forever."

She smiled politely. "Maybe for a little while, but not forever. We're actors, we belong on the stage, behind the darkness of the curtain, in the brightness of a thousand lights. I want to travel and see new places. Yes, this is beautiful, but there's more out there."

Were her words for his benefit or her own?

❧

OVER THE NEXT THREE WEEKS, CHARLES SPENT MOST OF HIS time with Grace, being the best gentleman he could.

They grew closer, as he hoped—knew—they would.

One night, after a very grueling day of rehearsals, involving some of the more difficult stunts, Grace sat in a heap on one of the oversized couches in the main cabin's great room. She was holding an ice pack to her left shoulder.

"Good God, Gracie? Are you all right?"

When they made eye-contact, hers were red-rimmed, like she was on the verge of tears. "Yeah, I'm good. Just sore." She shifted slightly and he could see the discomfort all over her face. Her eyebrows furrowed and her teeth clenched tight.

"Here." He touched her other shoulder. "Sit on the floor in front of me and let me see if I can help."

She slowly moved to the floor, complaining as she went. "Damn, it hurts just to move. Please don't do more damage."

"I won't."

He slowly worked out her shoulder muscles.

It was clear she'd never learned to do a stage fall before. Her body was paying for it.

She'd learn quick. Most actors did after one good, or bad in this case, kind of fall.

A fall that taught a lesson.

Grace had just been taught.

Charles smiled to himself as she moaned in pleasure.

She'd become so comfortable around him, allowing him to touch her intimately like this.

She'd even told him more about her past. Not much, but enough that he felt like she was really opening up.

"Oh, yeah... right there. Oh. Harder. Oh... my. Damn, boy. Your hands are made of magic. Can I keep them?" Her voice was husky, and his body reacted.

He needed to calm down.

Her words hit Charles hard.

"Can I keep them?"

Yes. And everything attached to them.

He needed to wait things out.
He had her right where he wanted her.
In twelve weeks, when the show had run its course...
Grace would be his.

THE END

Continued in Masquerade...

Also by Andrea Hurtt

Razor's Edge Rockstar Romance

Masquerade - Book 1

Undone - Book 1.5

Unmistakeable - Book 2

Incomplete - Book 3

Love Under Lockdown Series / Short Stories

Acting the Part in Lockdown

<u>Coming Soon</u>

Razor's Edge Rockstar Romance

Drowning - Book 4

Inconsolable - Book 5

The Sealgaire Saga

A Slice Of Hell - Book One

Prince Cove Curse

Under The Sea - Book One

About the Author

Andrea Hurtt is an emerging author of various romance categories. She enjoys writing a little bit of everything.

She's still deciding what she wants to be when she grows up. Andrea has been a dental assistant, a stay at home mom, owned her own clothing store, was a clothing designer with a vintage inspired clothing line, Amaryllis Designs, even won Omaha Fashion Week for Top Designer in her category, and Top Boutique for Cancer Survivor Night.

Pre-covid, Andrea spent her days either writing books or making #EmotionalSupportPillows and traveling around the USA and parts of Canada with the cast and fans of the CW TV show Supernatural.

Now she is on Canada, going to school for film and television, living out her life long dream of being an actress and screenwriter.

She is the mother of two children, two cats, one dog, and is a proud Army wife; currently residing in the MidWest, when not in school in Vancouver.

For more books and updates:
    www.pieceofpiepublishing.com
    www.facebook.com/andreahurttauthor
    www.Twitter.com/atomicbombshelı
    www.Instagram.com/AndreaHurttAuthor

Sneak Peek

Read on for an excerpt from

Andrea Hurtt's novel

Masquerade

See what happened to Grace and Charles

AVAILABLE NOW

Masquerade

"Maddie! Where's our Maddie?" The stage manager called for the star of the show, *her*.

As she stepped out onto the stage, enjoying the heat from the spotlight, Maddie took over. She fell in love with the boy-next-door her father had told her she could never have. As events unfolded, Maddie learned there was so much more out in the world.

The character went in search of something dangerous, something magical, only to discover she already had everything she desired in her own front yard.

Grace gave the performance of a lifetime—as she did at every single show.

She treated each performance as if it was the most important one of her life, because she never knew when it would be.

The cast took their applause and came back for the curtain call. The noise from the crowd was deafening.

If she did a thousand shows in her life, she'd still never get used to that sound. Her heart beat with the vibrations of the clapping. She felt so alive.

Her theater company was doing a US tour of their current

production, *The Splendids*. Their twelve-week run was almost over. They had two shows in Las Vegas, before finishing in Los Angeles.

She was so done with Vegas. Grace had stumbled during their last show. Disappointed with herself for her screw up, she didn't want to go out with the cast at the end of the night to meet fans.

She headed back to the hotel, where she could be alone.

Grace plopped down on the middle of the bed she shared with Maxine, one of the contortionists, fighting with tears she didn't want to shed.

A bag of Reese's Pieces, her comfort food, was staring at her from on top of her suitcase, like it knew she needed to cheer herself up. She sprung up to get the sugary sweetness.

She curled up on the floor, resting her back against the foot of the bed, pulling her knees up to her chest.

A knock on the door jarred her out of her head. The sense of passing time eluded her, but the bag of candy resting between her ankles was almost empty.

Grace looked at the door. Who could that be? None of the girls she shared with ever knocked. "Yes?" She called from the floor, not wanting to move.

"Grace? Are you all right?" The voice was muffled through the door, but it was Charles, her handsome, yet young, costar.

Over the past five months, they'd gotten to be close friends. She had to kiss him twice a day during productions, but that hadn't changed their friendship.

"Hold on," Grace called, doing her best not to spill the last of her candy, as she stood. She failed, and little hard shells tumbled around. She jumped over them. At least she hadn't crushed them into the carpet. She took a deep breath, letting it out in a huff before she opened the door.

Charles stared, his brown eyes intense, his shoulders pulled back in arrogance. "Really, Gracie? You're gonna hang out in your room and pout because you tripped? It happens. No one can be graceful all the time."

She laughed with her friend, tension loosening in her shoulders. He knew, better than anyone, how *un*graceful she was.

The only time she pulled off the illusion was when she was on stage.

"Yes, I'm gonna pout. But you might as well come pout with me. You screwed up too."

He stepped into the room, but didn't see the spilled Reese's on the floor. *Crunch crunch* under the soles of his boots had Grace whirling around.

She shoved him out of the way. "Stop! You're ruining my candy!" She squatted down to scoop up the salvageable pieces, popping some of them into her mouth.

"Ick! Grace! That's wrong! It's been on the floor."

"It's Reese's. The five-second rule applies."

"I think it's been over five-seconds."

"I don't care." Grace jumped on the bed and grinned.

Charles sat on the edge of the mattress, putting his hand on her knee. "So, back to what you said a second ago, about me screwing up. What the hell? I am always perfect."

"My ass! You laughed when I tripped. It was so out of character. Louis would've run to Maddie's side. *Not* laughed at her!"

As hard as she tried to be mad, he was right.

It was silly of her to beat herself up over it. A misplaced cord had caused her to trip, not something *she'd* done.

"Well, if I screw up next week, which I am sure will, you're allowed to laugh at me. Fair enough?" His expression said he was serious.

"Why do you think you'll mess up next week? As you said, you're perfect."

Charles wasn't perfect. He was very much a screwball when not performing. Their rehearsals were always so much fun because he messed around half the time. However, much like Grace; they let everything else go and allowed their characters to take over when they went on stage.

"My brother and some of his buddies are gonna be there."

"So?" she asked.

"So, I've always looked up to him. Like any little brother, all I've ever wanted was for him to be proud of me. This is my chance to show him what I've become, so I'm sure I'll screw it up." He smiled and patted her knee again before he ran that hand through his tousled blond hair. "I don't know which show he's coming to. He's busy, or so he says. But he guaranteed me he'd be at Saturday's Benefit Masquerade."

"Will you introduce me? I'd love to meet him."

"I guess. He's closer to your age. It still surprises me they got an old lady to play a teenager," he teased about their eight-year age difference.

"Old lady! Who're you calling an old lady?"

"You, of course."

She shoved at him, playfully, but hard, sending him crashing to the floor.

He landed with a great *humph*, followed by laughter.

Grace peered over the side of the bed.

He was still sitting on the floor. "Yeah, you and my brother will get along just fine. He likes to beat on me, too." Charles crawled back to the bed. "Everyone loves my brother." He sounded almost...sad. "Well, have a good one. I'd better go."

"Are you okay?"

"Yeah. Sure. See ya in the morning, Graceless," he called, and the door shut behind him.